Whoso sheddeth man's blood,
by man shall his blood be shed.
—Genesis 9:6

# To S. G.
*Fangs for everything.*

First U.S. paperback edition 1998

The Library of Congress has cataloged the hardcover edition as follows:

Anderson, M.T.
Thirsty / M.T. Anderson.—1st U.S. ed.
Summary: From the moment he knows that he is destined to
be a vampire, Chris thirsts for the blood of people around
him while also struggling to remain human.
ISBN 0-7636-0048-2 (hardcover)
[1. Vampires—Fiction. 2. Horror stories.] I. Title.
PZ7.A54395Th   1997
[Fic]—dc20      96-30744

ISBN 0-7636-0699-5 (paperback)

2 4 6 8 10 9 7 5 3 1

Printed in the United States of America

This book was typeset in Galliard.

Candlewick Press
2067 Massachusetts Avenue
Cambridge, Massachusetts 02140

# THIRSTY

## M.T. ANDERSON

CANDLEWICK PRESS
CAMBRIDGE, MASSACHUSETTS

IN THE SPRING, THERE ARE VAMPIRES IN THE WIND. People see them scuffling along by the side of country roads. At night, they move through the empty forests. They do not wear black, of course, but things they have taken off bodies or bought on sale. The news says that they are mostly in the western part of the state, where it is lonely and rural. My father claims we have them this year because it was a mild winter, but he may be thinking of tent caterpillars.

The bodies begin turning up in Springfield and Lenox and Williamstown. One is sitting slumped in the passenger seat of a Chevrolet pulled off on a dirt road. One man is found shoved into a closet on rows of well-buffed shoes, folded neatly like a wallet. One victim is barely buried. One is surrounded by swear words written in her own blood.

We are warned that the vampires look like normal people, except when they are angry or when the blood-lust is upon them.

One day in early April some people catch one just a few towns away, in Bradley. A policeman is wounded during the arrest, because a thirsty vampire has the strength of ten men.

We are very interested. It's all the local news talks about.

The annual Sad Festival of Vampires is coming up. It is an ancient festival in my hometown of Clayton held to keep Tch'muchgar, the Vampire Lord, locked in another world. It is said that the spirit Tch'muchgar in prehistoric times ravaged the land with an army of Darkness, and that his dominion extended over the whole expanse of mountain and forest now covered by the 508 and 413 area codes. It is said that it was he who then first laid the curse of vampirism on humans and made vampires live past death and suck the blood of the living.

It was for this that in ancient times the Forces of Light expelled him to a prison in another world and came in the form of shining beings to tell the Pompositticcut tribe what rituals should be done each year in special ritual sites to keep Tch'muchgar locked away forever. Nobody really believes much in Tch'muchgar anymore, but we still do the festival. Unfortunately, there is now a White Hen Pantry and a Texaco station standing on one of the ritual sites.

Last year, I went to the Sad Festival of Vampires with my two best friends, Tom and Jerk, and we watched the mayor and some local rabbis and priests do the festival in the White Hen. There was a big turnout. We saw the whole ritual, then Tom and I bought some Hood ice cream products and mashed them in the hood of Jerk's sweatshirt. That was a piece of subtle wordplay which Jerk only came to appreciate later.

Now it is almost time again for the Sad Festival of Vampires. There will be a fried chicken dinner at the firehouse, four dollars a plate, and there will be rituals in the White Hen Pantry, in the town forest, and in a boat out in the middle of the reservoir.

Maybe that will get rid of our vampire problem. Because there can be no doubt that they are on the move, and that they are stalking through forests and slipping across lawns. They are leaving behind them soft bodies, pale and limp. Sometimes after they kill, we are told, they cry, long and hard; sometimes they laugh.

"Come home before dark," my mother says.

And every night she hangs fresh garlic on the lintel of our front door, to guard against the vampires of spring.

☿

# CHAPTER 1

It is English, and I am watching Rebecca Schwartz's head.

It tilts down ten degrees and rotates slightly to the left. The sun catches it and turns her hair a more lustrous brown. Her hand is moving across the page, and loopy letters are following her pen. I am transfixed by this, even though I am supposed to be charting the syntax of a sentence about why people become flight attendants.

I think I have a crush on Rebecca Schwartz.

I haven't spoken to her much. I am in awe of her. It would be like Moses speaking to the burning bush. Whenever I go to speak with her, I feel like I should take off my shoes. I guess I am also pretty timid. I imagine speaking with her. Sometimes I construct whole conversations where we say unusual things to each other.

I picture us walking through the forest in the spring. This is not a particularly original fantasy, I know. For one thing, it is in about every personal ad Tom and I have ever read. "SWM," they say, "seeking SWF, non-smoker who enjoys long walks in the forest, quiet evenings by the fire, and strolls by the sea." People are not very original when it comes to romance. I think that's too bad. Sometimes you want to see a personal ad that says, "SWM seeking SWF, nonsmoker who enjoys flailing in pig poop, puking, and honking on bagpipes.

Women who do not know 'My Lassie Yaks in Bonny Mull' need not apply."

But I am not in the mood for pig poop today; so instead, I kiss her in the forest. There is sun and lots of mosquitoes.

I look up from my diagram and see her face rotated at one quarter as she looks toward the clock. I feel awful for having thought about kissing her. It is after the time when the bell should ring. I tap my pencil three times on the desk impatiently.

I look down. I draw a stem for the prepositional phrase to sit on. I clearly and deliberately write down "to many satisfied airline passengers."


The bell rings and we are going out of the room into the hall, where there is banging and shouting. I quickly try to maneuver toward Rebecca and her friends because she is talking to Tom, who knows her better than I do. I angle a few steps in that direction. They are heading for the lunchroom. I wade toward them. Suddenly Jerk appears at my side. He is as big as a roadblock. His hand-me-down pants are too short for his legs.

I am thinking desperately of things to say to her.

Jerk is in repellently high spirits. "Chris! Hey, Chris, I thought that would never end. I thought—did you get number four?" He squints. "That was the one with the guy who had a layover in Newark. It was real hard."

I say curtly, "The hardest." Jerk is unwelcome right now. I am considering my conversational options with Rebecca.

"It was so boring!" Jerk is still exclaiming. "So boring! Boring, boring, boring!"

"Let's go over and talk to Tom," I say carefully. I push in that direction. They are moving down the hall. I am keenly aware that, conversationally, appearing with Jerk in his happy-to-see-you mode is like taking a dead moose as carryon luggage.

"More boring," he adds cheerfully, "than a *very boring thing* from the planet Tedium."

Tom, Rebecca, and the rest have reached the stairs. They are going down. I am estimating whether I can reach them in time. Jerk keeps pace with me.

"Hey, Chris!" exclaims Jerk. "Isn't that your brother? Waving to you?" He gestures down the hall away from the stairs. My brother is there, waving to me.

I swear and move in the opposite direction. No time to lose.

"Chris!" I hear my brother shouting over the din.

"It's your brother!" Jerk says, tugging at my arm.

"Really, Jerk? I guess that would explain why he sleeps and eats in my house." Rebecca and Tom and the others have disappeared down the stairs.

My big brother, Paul, works his way through the lunchtime crowd to me. He is short for his age, so he has to bounce up to see me over everyone else. He tugs on opposite sides of his sweatshirt hood drawstring. "Chris!" he says to me.

"What do you want?" I say.

"Tonight," he says. "What we're doing is going to the lynching."

"What?" I say.

"The lynching," he explains, shifting carefully to let someone bigger pass. "A vampire. I'm going to go over to Bradley tonight to see them, like, stake the undead."

"You aren't."

"After Mom and Dad leave."

"Chris —," Jerk begins, turning toward me.

"Where are Mom and Dad going?" I ask Paul.

"Out to dinner. And I have to keep you with me, slimestick. Mom said that I do. We'll go out, and if she calls, we went to Mark's house. We'll be gone for maybe, like, an hour."

"Chris," says Jerk, "if we stay here, all the tater tots will be gone by the time we get there."

"You're going to drag me over to Bradley to watch a lynching?" I say hotly. "It's not like they're going to do it out in front of everybody. It'll be in the courthouse."

He shakes his head. "I'm there, Chris. All the media and everything are going to be there. Some girls from school are going to be there. I will be there. And Mom is, like, Miss Hyper, so you will be there."

"You are just trying to assert yourself because you're only half an inch taller than I am," I say.

"I am not."

"I'll get a ruler."

"Asserting myself."

"I just don't believe you," I say, disgusted.

Paul shakes his head. "I am not going to argue about this, butthole."

I shrug my shoulders. I head toward the lunchroom.

He's been a pain to me and to everyone since his girl-friend figured out that he is a geek and dropped him like a tarantula casserole.

When I reach the lunchroom, the others—Tom and Rebecca and her friends—have already found a table and have sat down. They are talking a lot and laughing at Tom's jokes. He gestures as part of some story and makes a face like a Gila monster.

I pass by their table and look for a way that I might be able to slip in on the end or maybe on one of the cor-ners. I am about to set the tray down in a cramped space when Jerk says over my shoulder, "It's too crowded. There are some seats over there."

Rebecca looks up at me and has heard it. She elevates her slim neck.

I am feeling guilty for having tried to ditch Jerk, so now I can't. We go and sit together, far away from the others. You have to feel bad for him, after all. I feel bad because we all call him Jerk, and he is not the person with the highest self-esteem in the whole world.

"Wait until Tom hears you're going to the lynching,"

says Jerk. "He'll be so jealous, he'll be chewing on two-by-fours."

"Two-by-fours," I say, staring at my tater tots. "I'm not sure I follow you."


A year and a half ago my mother and father informed us that as soon as we go away to college, they are getting a divorce. They are waiting.

After their big fight they avoided each other. My father worked late nights at the Staticom laboratory. My mother watched television or called her real-estate clients. Things were very bad for a year. Now, though, they are eating dinner at the same time and sleeping in the same room again, and they recognize each other by sight. They do not like to fight in front of Paul and me, ever since they overheard us referring to them as Ward and June. Now they go out to dinner alone once a month to fight.

Paul is a year older than me, so he can drive. He and his friend Mark are both into video and the media, so they jump at any chance to try and be on TV. Mark was in a crowd on the news once before, after the street near the dam flooded. You could distinctly see him behind the police cordon, waving.

They are in the front seat, and I am in the back seat. I can't hear much of what they're saying over the radio. It's techie talk about the lighting booth in the school auditorium. While they talk Mark keeps on idly making zoom-lens motions with his hands, testing out angles and shots for the camera of the imagination. As usual, Mark's hair is everywhere and curly. Paul is driving. He got his driver's license recently, so he is at some stage where he constantly talks to people driving around him. "Uh-dur, ma'am!" he says. "Rotary? Right of way?"

We pass along through the avenue of pines by the reservoir's edge. The evening has not turned the sky dark yet. The trees stand out against the clouds.

We are almost out of the town. We pass a series of slanted fields.

Because I cannot hear Paul and Mark, I sit back in the seat and think what if I were going to the lynching with real friends, really cool ones who don't necessarily exist. I picture us taut with excitement and dressed in black. We are talking about the meaning of oppression; my twenty-five-year-old girlfriend is staring moodily out the window. One of my friends has brought his sketch-book because he wants to catch the lineaments of human depravity and also pain and suffering. This is what artists do sometimes.

We are on Route 495. Mark is flipping between radio stations.

"Where are we going to park?" says my brother. "All the spaces near the courthouse are going to be taken."

Mark is leaning down to peer at the radio display. "There are some places at Cumberland Farms," he says.

"But you have to be a patron."

"Look at this asshole," says my brother. "It's often customary to drive in a lane."

"Where did they find the last body?" Mark asks, focusing his invisible camera on his reflection in the darkening windows.

Paul stops to wait for a red light. "I think on the roof of the hardware store over on the other side of town. Near the Hudson line. Nice turn signal, buttlick."

We go to McDonald's. I order a double hamburger, six-piece McNuggets, and a medium fries. I have been very hungry lately. We drive into the center of town. We go past the Cumberland Farms parking lot, because it is full. People are already clustered around the courthouse, yelling and shouting. Police lights are flashing in the gloaming.

We park in front of the Bradley House of Pizza and get out. Paul starts to pay the meter and Mark reminds him that it is after six and that he is a moron. I feel stupid carrying my McDonald's bag, and my fingers are all sticky from the fries. I shift from foot to foot and chew. At the Bradley House of Pizza, there is a sign in the tattered plate glass window, "Making your favorite sub for forty years!" Talk about slow service.

We head down to the mob. Everyone is still relatively pleasant. The police are putting up orange sawhorses to keep a clear path up the steps of the courthouse. People are chatting. A woman who dressed in a sleeveless pink top when the sun was up is rubbing her upper arms and shivering. "Oh god, I know," she says to her friend.

Vampires are lynched, traditionally. It is too costly to hold them for trial. A full-grown vampire is immortal if well fed, but can't live long without human blood; and it is tricky to come by donors. There's no need for a trial, I guess, because there's not much doubt about vampires. There are, after all, the pointy teeth and the mirror problems. Whenever their blood-lust is upon them, their fangs slide forward, and they have no reflection to speak of. And once people find those signs, it's all over for the vampire. If you are a vampire and still alive, people know you must be guilty of murder. There's no other alternative—no other way you could live. So sometimes they will burn you. Usually they will drive a stake through your heart.

We wait. As the evening grows darker, the crowd gets larger and sounds angrier. The police who are waiting look around nervously and occasionally consult one another. One of them is sitting in the squad car, muttering into the CB.

People stare at me as I dip my McNuggets into the barbecue sauce. The pieces keep sticking in my throat. I want to finish them as quickly as possible.

I crumple up the recycled bag and throw it in a rusty barrel. Mark and Paul have made their way through the crowd to the news vans, where technicians are setting up lights and a camera crew is connecting wires.

We hear sirens a long way off. Everyone starts to fall silent. I scuffle my shoe on the pavement and look for something to stand on. A father has picked up his little daughter and perched her on his shoulders. The police are walking up and down the lines of sawhorses, asking people to step back from the barriers. The news cameras are ready, and technicians are squinting into the viewfinders.

The police escort arrives, sirens blaring. Everyone is staring.

The doors open and police hurry out, surrounding the car. Some hold pistols aimed at something inside. A cluster of officers surrounds the back left door, and they are taking someone out.

The vampire is a young woman, or at least she looks young. She is fair haired, and her hands are bound behind her by cuffs on a heavy metal bar. The crowd moves forward to see; she glares sideways at them. They press against the barriers. The police run up and down, motioning them back. People are screaming foul names at her, calling her a murderer and a witch. Some high-school kids are holding up a little mirror, slanting it, ducking to try to see if they can catch her reflection. "You bitch!" one man is screaming at her, bellowing so loud he leans across the barrier. "You bitch!" On the other side, an old woman is crying, sobbing—"My baby! My baby!" Two police officers are holding the old woman back, and I do not know whether her baby is a victim or the vampire herself.

The vampire stumbles up the steps. She is being pushed by one of the policemen. Someone throws an empty Coke can and it bounces softly off her head.

She turns on the highest step and looks at us. She gazes across the crowd, her mouth tight and closed.

Then she looks at me. She is staring at me.

I turn around to see if there's someone gesturing or someone who's caught her attention, but she is staring just at me.

She knows me.

For a moment we pause there. Her eyes scrape from one side of my face to the other, registering a cool kind of hatred and an accusation.

She looks like she wants to say something, to shout something.

She starts to raise her hand as if to point.

We stand there, staring at each other, for a moment. She moves her lips.

However, she does not want to show her teeth before the crowd. She is proud. She keeps her lips closed, drops her hand, and turns to go inside to her last death.

She goes in. The doors swing shut behind her.

She is gone.


The police say there is nothing more to see.

My brother is complaining that the lynching was anticlimactic because it was held behind closed doors.

He says that there was nothing to it and that the news blew it out of proportion into a big sob story.

"She knew who I was," I say gravely.

Paul doesn't understand me. He says, "It doesn't take much to know a buttplug."


When we get home, Mom and Dad are back. The dinner did not go well.

"It went great," says my mother. "Especially when your father charged it to his credit card and it was refused."

"That's not fair, honey," my father says.

They start yelling at each other, and Paul and I step away silently and go upstairs to our rooms. Downstairs my father is saying, "You didn't have to say it in front of the kids, sugar."

"Don't you call me sugar! Don't! Or honey!" my mother protests.

My father should have known better than to call her a condiment. You have to earn the right to call my mother a condiment.

But later I can hear them going to the same bedroom to sleep, as I lie awake. I can hear them as I stare at the ceiling. They are getting into their bed.

I can hear them breathing and my mother snoring. I am the only one awake.

My head is under the pillow.

For a few months now, I have been feeling hungrier and hungrier. Food does not seem to fill me up.

"Got a hollow leg?" my mother asks.

At night, I have been especially hungry. Sometimes I can't sleep well because I'm so hungry. Also, I have been feeling strange little percolations in my chest. Whatever it is, I don't like it. It's a desire for something, but I can't tell what. It makes me uncomfortable sometimes during the day. It has been disturbing my sleep occasionally at night. It is like a leaping or a squelching or an anguish about nothing at all. Maybe it's love, these percolations, that's what I think.

But maybe it's not love at all.

That night, after the lynching, after I am recognized by one of the damned, the hunger is very bad.

I lie with my head under the pillow.

Everyone else is asleep.


I dream of a straight road. It is night, and my headlights define a row of beeches.

I stop at a crosswalk where there's a single flashing yellow light. A fair-haired woman starts to cross.

She makes it halfway across before she turns and peers through the windshield.

Her look is of fury and hatred.

She is the vampiress.

She crosses; and I drive on, shaken.

At the next crosswalk, I pull to a halt. She crosses again. When she reaches the halfway point, she turns and stares at me.

I do not know if I have murdered her and she is haunting me.

I am wrapped in her arms, my face buried in her neck. I feel the softness of her breasts against my chest and move my hands up toward them.

"Do not worry," she croons. "You are mine."

*You are mine.*

# CHAPTER 2

To make the Wompanoag Reservoir, they flooded two towns on purpose. It is the kind of thing that would be embarrassing to do by accident.

They arranged for great walls and trestles to be thrown up and aqueducts to pass through the forest.

They evacuated two little villages and paid some people to live somewhere else. Then at the time appointed, someone closed the sluice gates, and the river slowly rose and covered miles of the valley. The water crawled up tree trunks and ate steeples and hymnbooks and empty drawers. People say that there are still two towns under the reservoir. It is a strange idea, eels and sunfish hanging in windows and bedrooms.

The town of Clayton dribbles down the slopes of a deep valley on either side of the river. The whole town—the white houses, the new Catholic church, the old brick Victorian factories—faces the white wall of the dam. When we were younger, Tom and I used to talk about what it would be like if the dam disappeared and there were a huge tidal wave. We talked about it covering the school and leaving only the drifting oil from Cindy Brandt's big hair.

Huge square buildings of granite and marble are spaced around the dam and the shores of the lake. They are like tombs or maybe whited sepulchers. In fact they are water purification plants and well houses, and I think one of them is a pump. They have made a park on one side of the reservoir with grass and paths. Leading across the still river and up a hill are the giant trestles that used to support the aqueduct. Now they are just columns, and they support pieces of the air.

We are walking down the precipitous steps. On some trees, the buds are out. On others, they are just a sort of red fuzz.

I want to talk to Tom alone about some things, mainly things like feeling strange wild thirsts and longings in your chest when the evening falls, and what to do about desire, but it's difficult to bring that kind of thing up just after lunch. I want to know what I should do about Rebecca, and whether the hopping, giddy feeling I have is love; I want to know why I'm having trouble sleeping sometimes and what this strange hunger is. And I want to ask Tom because Tom knows Rebecca better than I do, and he is better looking than I am. We can sit by the shores of the obsidian lake and talk of whether I am in love.

"Then Choi goes into the central torture chamber," says Tom. "There are all these people with hypodermics stuck into them and stuff. There's this guy with nunchaks."

"I don't understand the hypodermics," I say.

"Like shots," says Tom.

"No," I say, "why are they in the torture chamber?"

"Because they're injecting people with heroin or something."

"Later in the movie, did you see the scene with the truck?" asks Jerk from behind us.

I am bored. I keep looking around and fantasizing that we will run into Rebecca Schwartz on the buzzed grass.

Tom is saying, "So the guy with the nunchaks starts spinning them around in front of his face and so on, like, showing off."

This could go on for some time.


Tom and Jerk are my two best friends, I guess.

When we were younger, we used to spend the afternoons running around in the woods together and we stayed over at one another's houses and all. Late at night, after watching *Twilight Zone* reruns on cable, we'd look out the windows at the stars and have wide-eyed, frightened conversations about whether there was a God. Once, when Tom's parents had his grandmother taken off to a home, after she went insane and kept breaking dishes and saying that the Lord would make whole what was sundered, Jerk and I went over to Tom's house and invited him to go walking, and we all talked seriously about the whole thing and then told some dumb jokes and we all laughed, and later Tom thanked us for being such good friends. And Tom did the same for me when my grandfather died. So we have been friends for years.

We first called Jerk Jerk back when he was shorter than us. First us, then everybody else. Now he is much taller, even though he stoops to try to apologize for it. His name is Michael Polinsky. At least, that's what he writes at the top of his papers.

Tom is slim, though not as slim as I am, and girls think he's cute. He often reminds me of this. He doesn't have braces. I have had braces since I was ten. Tom and I have been friends for at least that long. In some ways, out of the two, I am starting to prefer the braces.

Tom and I have been friends mainly because he has always had an imagination of some sort and so have I, I'd like to think. We pretended a lot of things a few years ago, back when we were into pretending.

Recently I have been noticing that his imagination isn't really as good as I thought it was. It mainly revolves around things just being louder and more explosive than they really are. He'll say things like, "What if you had this car, and it went five hundred miles an hour and shot flames out the tailpipe?" There is really no answer to that kind of question. The speed limit is fifty-five in Massachusetts anyway.

I picture myself with different friends. They are artists and dress in black, and we say cool things to one another and laugh about wrecking slick cars. I don't know anyone like that, but I want to. Instead, I have to hear dumb plot synopses for B movies involving nunchaks and helicopters. Recently, I have found myself wanting to talk about more serious things with Tom. Instead, even though I know he must think about serious things, somehow we always end up talking about more nunchak movies, with maybe a brief break for a cat-o'-nine-tails. Sometimes I want to say, "Tom, enough cats-o'-nine-tails. Can we talk about something that doesn't cause internal bleeding?"

But I don't want to offend him; and I don't want him to know that I am confused and don't know what to do. I don't want him to know about these new feelings of unrest in the evenings, unless, as I suspect, he feels them, too.


The sky is moving along quickly. I am nonsensically scanning the crags and paths for Rebecca, because I always feel like I might meet her here. Far in the distance, a man in black is walking toward us. The brown grassland by the shore rises up to the woods. Tom is still telling me about the combat. Choi has now been pinned to a metal table and they're bringing a drill toward his face.

"So he grabs this gun—," Jerk adds.

"It's on the table right next to him," explains Tom. "The other guy forgot about it completely."

"Who grabs the gun?" I say, uninterested.

"Choi, duh," says Tom. "The other guy has the drill."

"Well, it's not like you can only have one weapon in life," I explain.

"Well, it's not like you can only have one brain cell in life," says Tom.

"Sorry," I say. To our right are rows of bottlebrush pines. The shadows of the stark sun on the limbs blotch and stripe the bark. The man in black is getting closer.

"Who are you looking for?" Tom asks, squinting toward the trees.

I shrug nervously. "I'm not looking for anybody. I have never looked for fewer people in my life."

I stop looking for Rebecca.

"Did you tell him," says Jerk, "the part about the truck? Tell him about the truck."

I feel like I am going to go insane.


I do not know how to explain why you have a crush on someone. I have a crush on Rebecca, but I cannot explain why I do because I do not know her well. When I think about it and ask myself about it, what comes to me are incidents. There was a hot summer night last year when I saw her at Persible Dairy, which is an ice cream stand. It was very hot that night, so no one could sleep.

She was in a summer dress, but she wore no shoes. Her feet arched and flinched on the warm gravel. She and her twenty-year-old sister were walking toward their hot, ticking car, talking.

"Shut up," her sister said, laughing, "and eat your ice cream."

"There are seven paths to wisdom," Rebecca continued, raising her cone to her lingering tongue, "but I think the first three are smelly."

She did a pirouette, and I saw her pockets were stuffed with napkins.

The afternoon drags on. We are talking and walking by the shore.

I have not yet thought of a way to lose Jerk. I can't just say "Go home" or offer him ten dollars. If he weren't with us, he wouldn't have anything to do all afternoon. He would sit around and mope and watch *Creature Double Feature*. I cannot say anything serious in front of him, though, because he will offer some of his embarrassing advice. "Why not try different shoe sizes?"

As we cross a thin bridge over the dam's rapids and eye the rusty cogs and ratchets of yesteryear, the two of them tell me the truck episode from the Choi movie. It is long and involves some chains and a busty blonde woman.

"That's just like *The Hitcher*," I say. "That happens at the end."

We watch the man in black stalk toward us, taking the high path, stepping along it with a purposeful stride.

"That was a great flick," says Jerk.

"It was," I agree dully. "There was a truck scene like that at the end. Where he's about to pull the woman in half by taking his foot off the brake pedal."

"I saw it with Kristen Mosley," says Tom.

"I am getting sick of seeing women pulled apart in horrible ways," I say.

"On video," adds Tom.

"Yes," I agree, "I can never tire of it in real life."

"No," says Tom. "I saw it with Kristen Mosley on video. Sort of saw it. Needless to say, there were a couple of things that interfered with my concentration."

I walk on for a minute, following the soft tawny shoulder of grass around the rim of the lake. The sneering pride in Tom's voice is ringing through my head.

"It was a wicked good film," says Jerk, "but a little bloody. Bloodier than a very bloody thing from the planet Hemorrhage."

I turn to Tom and challenge him suddenly. "What did you mean? What did you mean you *sort of* saw it?" I ask, even though I know the answer.

Tom slows a step. He looks at me slyly and answers, "You know. There we were, on the couch."

The wind has risen. Little whitecaps catch on the lake. "I don't believe you said that," I say.

With a glint of calculation in his eye, he boldly adds, "Two big wobbly diversions."

I am suddenly irritated. He is doing this to irritate me. "I don't believe you're telling us this," I say.

"What's your problem?" says Tom, still looking at me boldly. The man in black approaches.

"I'm serious," I say to Tom nervously. "I can't believe you're so cocky. Can't you see it's embarrassing?"

"For you, maybe," says Tom.

"Are you boasting?" I ask.

"I have something to boast about. You're hyper. What the hell is your problem?"

"I do not have a problem," I say. "My problem is the fact that you're doing this male boob-boast maneuver."

Tom keeps pace with me. He is smirking. The wind waps his hair. "They're sort of like Nintendo," he presses. "You get bored pretty quick if you own a set, but it's fun to go over and play with a friend's. Bet you ten bucks that guy in black's a CIA agent."

"Screw this," I say harshly. "You're talking like a . . ." Whatever I am going to say is stupid and prissy, so I do not say it.

"You're so goddamn jealous!" he says. "What's your problem?"

"Stop it, you two," says Jerk.

But Tom insists, "Lately you are always having a problem. You are being a complete peckerhead."

"I am not a peckerhead," I protest.

"Medical evidence suggests—"

"Would you shut up? I just want to—I don't know." I am not going to say a thing about girls. That will feed his ego.

"For about three weeks," says Tom, now slightly hot, "you've been acting like this."

"Like what?"

"Like a jerk. Pardon the expression. For about three weeks you've been acting like an asshole. You've been jumping down our throats. You've been saying weird things. I don't know what's up with you. You have more goddamn baggage than Grand Central Station."

I say bitterly, "Here we go."

Tom is saying, "Look, Chris. I don't want to take your shit just because you want to feel up Rebecca goddamn Schwartz."

I stare at him. I can feel the blood shoot up to my face. Birds are wheeling in the trees. "How did you know?" I ask.

"What do you mean? It's not some state secret. What's your problem? You never talk to her, you stutter when you try, it's just a crush."

"You haven't told her, have you?" I say. I hope to sound rough, but I sound squeaky.

"Who needs telling?" he asks. "You're being pathetic. Just ask her out. It's not like she's some hot sex goddess with the biggest tits in history."

"And I apologize for thinking of her in exactly that way," I say.

"I'm serious, man," says Tom. Jerk is standing a bit apart, staring at us warily. "You should just ask her out. What's stopping you? The worst thing that can happen is she laughs at you for months and it becomes this big urban legend."

So I ask, "You think I should?"

Tom looks at me and starts to smile. "You're fishing for compliments," he says. "Aren't you?" He is looking slightly malicious. "What do you want me to say?"

I answer, "Nothing," and turn away. The man in black is quite close to us now. His suit coat ruffles in the wind.

"What do you want me to say?" prods Tom. "If you want me to say that you're good looking, you have another goddamn thing coming."

"I didn't say that."

"I'm not going to lie."

The man in black steps along, slim and tall, a knowing smile on his lips. His black leather shoes are wet from the grass.

"I appreciate your honesty," I say bitingly.

"Chris, you're nothing to write home about, buddy," says Tom mildly. "But remember, you have your gargantuan intellect and biting wit. Look at that guy's suit. Got to be a CIA agent. You gentlemen owe me ten dollars."

"It wasn't a bet," says Jerk glumly. "We didn't shake on it."

"I wasn't fishing for compliments," I say. "I know I'm not great looking."

"Hello, boys," the man says. He passes us.

Tom shrugs. "Look, Chris. Seriously. You're not a

monster," he says. "You're better looking than a lot of people." He pauses, and blurts, "Like burn victims." He laughs out loud. "Sorry," he says.

"Thanks for your support," I say.

Tom demands, "What?"

"You really can be a bastard," I say.

He looks at me. "Why?" he sneers. "Because I could peg Rebecca Schwartz to the floor in my sleep?"

That is it.

I feel a violent urge. I do not know where it comes from. I am grappling with him, and he has fallen back on the grass. "You bastard!" I am saying. I am saying it again and again. I feel strangely strong. I want something terrible to happen to him. My mouth is watering.

For a moment, we perch there. My knee pins his stomach. The waves are lapping on the shore. I look at the water. The man in black has heard us shout. He turns back toward us. Slowly, he points his finger.

My eyes swoop down and hit the lake. There, beside Tom's shoulder, they rest on the water.

It is then that I see that I have no reflection.

I see the clouds behind my head. I see Tom's shoulder hanging out over the water. I look down and see our legs, lying in the mud. His are reflected; mine are not.

"You are so full of shit," he says, seeing how I've frozen.

When he pushes me off, I lie there, staring sideways at the water. I will not say anything to him about it. I desperately want to blurt, "I'm not in the water!" But I won't. I won't tell him. It is probably just some trick of the light. I need to stop and stare and see what trick of the light it is. All I need to do is bend my head a different way.

I watch Tom swear and wring out the cuff of his jeans.

Jerk is fussing around us. "Are you okay? Are you, like, okay? Hey, what—?"

"Come on," says Tom.

I watch their legs walk away over the grass. Tom's dry foot and wet foot going plod, squoosh, plod, squoosh.

I wait for a minute. The plod, squoosh fades to nothing. Then I roll over so that my head is projecting out over the water.

I watch and breathe shallowly. Nothing at first. Then, slowly, slowly, I watch my face reappear in the reservoir.

For a while I lie like that, my leg in the mud, my face hanging a few inches above the ripples that, just a few moments before, would not hold my image.


A figure is bending over me. The man in black is at my side. He reaches down one of his fine hands and pulls me to my feet.

His face is hard and young and almost elfin. Though he is wearing a sharp sixties suit, it looks as if he could play the panpipe and worship things among the toadstools.

He has a compassionate smile, though. "I saw what happened," he says.

I look at him. I am sort of wary, because I am not quite sure what happened.

"How they ganged up on you," he says.

I shrug, and I say, "I started it."

He nods, and his hair moves in the wind. He puts his hands in his pockets. "Did you? Did you start it? Who can say? You are going through a difficult age," he says, "I'm sure. So many contrary emotions. Some of them very new and violent. You won't be a boy for long. There are a lot of changes you're going through right now. Hormonal and so on."

"Yes," I say. I want to escape. One of my feet steps toward Tom and Jerk, who are getting farther and farther away. I can tell Tom is mimicking me, and Jerk is nodding sadly.

The man in black squints down the shore at them. Then, with a wide smile, he adds suddenly, "You must feel very disoriented sometimes."

"Yes," I mumble. I want to run and rejoin Tom and Jerk, because if I don't rejoin them soon, Tom will not forgive me. Instead of forgiving me, he will employ his Five-Alarm Sarcasm, which has been known to strip the finish off Colonial furniture.

The clouds can be seen moving on the surface of the water.

"I saw you the other night at the lynching," says the

young man, rocking on his heels. "You seemed surprised. Startled? Uneasy?"

I nod.

"I saw her die," he says, looking above my left shoulder out at the lake, biting his upper lip for a moment in regret. "The stake didn't go in correctly. It was too large to fit through her ribs. As the executioner pounded it in, you could hear the ribs popping and cracking." He looks at me. "Watching a vampire die, the worst part is the heart. It's acquired a life of its own by that time. When the stake reaches the heart, the heart starts squealing in terror. Like a piglet."

"That's . . . of . . . okay. Thanks," I mutter. "I guess I better catch up with my friends." I start to walk away.

Tom and Jerk are now far away, walking shoulder to shoulder. I would stay and talk to this man, who I can see has an unusual and stimulating viewpoint, except that he is obviously a psychopath and I'm not yet interested in dying. (LOCAL BOY FOUND DECAPITATED IN DITCH: "MISSING HEAD NOT MUCH OF A LOSS," SAYS EX-FRIEND TOM.) I am walking away down the path of yellow grass.

"I saw the whole fight just now," the man in black is repeating behind me.

I keep walking.

"I saw what you saw," he says.

I keep walking.

"I saw that you had no reflection in the lake."

I stop. Chills go up and down my spine.

I turn back to him.

"No reflection." He has stepped back and is sitting down casually on the embankment. "Don't worry. I've been sent to help you."

"What?" I say. "Help?"

"I am an avatar of the Forces of Light."

"What?" I say stupidly.

"I'm a celestial being. I've been sent to ask your help. Must I shout, Christopher?" I walk back warily to his side.

"How do I know that you're a celestial being?" I ask. "You don't look anything like a celestial being to me."

He rolls his eyes and smiles a disappointed little smile. Then he wavers and flickers like a flame on the wind. He disappears and reappears.

When he is fully substantial again, I say to him, "I guess you are a celestial being."

"You see?"

"Um, you have two left hands now."

He swears and switches his hand back. "That should be ample proof, in any case," he says. Out of his pocket he takes a pair of designer sunglasses with thin horn rims. He puts them on. "We in the Forces of Light are worried about you, Christopher."

I stare at him. "What?" I say.

"We're worried because you're going to become a vampire."

"What? No."

"Yes. You know it. You are—"

x

"No, I'm not."

"Yes, you are."

"No. That was just a trick of the light, and—"

"Yes, Christopher. Yes." He nods, slowly and finally. He has held up both his hands for silence, like he's about to cue an invisible ghost orchestra playing cow-skull fiddles. He repeats gently, pleadingly, "Yes, Christopher."

"But I'm not dead." I am backing away from him, feeling a little sick and panicked. I realize I keep touching my cheek with my finger. "I can't be a vampire. I'm not dead."

"Vampirism is a lonely highway, and there are many routes that lead there," he says. "Stop moving backward. Some vampires were cursed after they died; some were born with the curse, passed on from their parents; some were cursed while still alive. You have the curse in you. I don't know why. But puberty has set it off within you. Hormones. In a few months—four, I'd say, at the outside—you're going to be fully vampiric. You're going to need blood to survive. I said stop moving backward. You're about to trip over a hummock."

"Where did I get the curse?"

"I said I don't know. I'm sorry." He folds his hands in front of him. "That is not the question. The question is what you're going to do now. You have to think of your health. Vampires heal almost instantaneously. They're very hard to kill for this reason. You will stop aging in a few years, and you will be immune to disease. But it

**43**

remains a sad little irony—this is an irony you will find very sad, Christopher—the sad irony is that most vampires die very quickly. You can be killed with a stake through the heart if you are caught. Or you can starve to death if you don't drink human blood. That's a tall order, drinking human blood. You will have to kill to live."

"I've got to go," I babble. "I have to catch up with my friends." I gesture wildly toward Jerk and Tom.

The celestial being's gaze shifts and he focuses on them. Far down the shore, Jerk is chasing pigeons. He makes roaring noises and waves his arms at them. He is so far away it sounds like he is mewling like a kitten.

I say apologetically, "They may not be much, but they are the only friends I have."

The celestial being in the sharp black suit smiles quickly at me. "I try hard," he says, "to love every human soul."

He folds his hands in his lap. "May I continue? Please, Christopher, don't try to run away from this. I told you that I'm here to help you. Do you understand? Help."

"How can you help me?"

"You, Christopher, are on the cusp. You may move through both human and vampiric society with impunity. To humans, you are a human; to vampires, a vampire. In a few months, that will not be the case."

"Why?" I ask. "What will the case be?"

"Since you ask about the case, I'll tell you. You'll be too savage and crazy to fit in among the human population. To the vampires, if you haven't killed, you'll still be too human to run with them. Human, meaning reluctant to stalk people and suck their blood."

The sky is graying. The lake looks like granite. "I'm not going to stalk any people," I protest, almost tripping over the words. "I'm not that kind of person."

The celestial being looks at me with eyes invisible behind his dark designer glasses. He tells me, "You know what I am talking about. You know you are becoming a vampire. The vampiress recognized it in you. Vampires can see other vampires. And you don't reflect when the blood-lust is upon you. You saw it in the lake."

"I don't know—"

"Water doesn't lie." He still stares at me. "Your thirst is only beginning now. When you get angry, you become vampiric. And vice versa. When you get thirsty, you get angry without reason. Increasingly. You feel prone to violence. You feel prone to drink blood. In four months, your blood-thirst will have overwhelmed you. You won't be able to control yourself for long."

"I don't have to listen to this," I say. "This is all the completest bullshit. I bet you're not a celestial being at all."

"I am too a celestial being. Christopher, I can help you. If you help the Forces of Light and act as a secret spy in the ranks of the damned, then we guarantee that we will cure you one hundred percent of the fatal scourge of vampirism."

He waits. "And if you don't," he adds with quiet

simplicity, "in five months you'll be dead. This is not a threat; it is the truth. Either you will not have killed, in which case you'll die of starvation, or you will have killed and been caught and lynched. Holy water to sear and blind you. A stake in your chest to finish you off."

"What if I'm not turning into a vampire?"

"You are turning into a vampire. Don't doubt it."

We remain there for a moment. I am standing, with mud drying on my shoe. He is sitting, with the grass blowing around him. I feel like I cannot hear my own thoughts. Inside my head it is silent. The sky is getting darker.

"You have heard of Tch'muchgar?" he asks me suddenly.

"The Vampire Lord?"

"Yes. That's the very one."

"It's not a common name," I say, shrugging.

"No," he agrees. "I can tell it is going to be a pleasure to work with you. Now consider Tch'muchgar: blasted from this world in man's prehistory by the Forces of Light, snared in the most potent of enchantments for his grotesque misdeeds, and imprisoned in a foreign world that happens to have one of its points of entrance underneath this fine municipal reservoir. This is all true as you've heard it. Also very real are the spells that yearly must be cast here and in the White Hen Pantry off Route 62.

"This summer, Tch'muchgar will try to escape. He is

locked in a parallel world—unable to move even a fraction, unable to see, seething with hatred. You see, we in the Forces of Light do not kill. It is a rule of ours: No death by our hands. Sometimes the greater punishment is to let something live.

"Though Tch'muchgar technically has no power in this world, he has managed to stain certain impressions on the minds of his vampiric servants. Vampires are loners, but he's convinced them to work together. The plan is that this summer, during your Sad Festival of Vampires, they will interrupt the spells of binding that your towns-people cast yearly to hold Tch'muchgar; they will interrupt the spells just when those bonds are being reforged and are at their most delicate. Then the Vampire Lord will return, burst back into the world, and chaos will ensue."

"What do you mean?"

"I think I've been very clear so far, Christopher. Tch'muchgar the Vampire Lord will return and probably conquer most if not all of North America. Then he will most likely start to use mankind as cattle. Keep a few around as studs to corral and breed. Cripple their children. Lock each one in its dark little cubbyhole for easy storage until it starts to mature. Keep the race fed on a protein-rich diet. Then kill them, one by one, and drink their blood."

I shuffle from one leg to the other.

"Okay," I say. "And me?"

"And you what?"

"What do you want me to do?"

The celestial being draws his fingers ticklingly along the bottom side of his jaw. Then he drops his hand to his lap again and nods. "As I've said, you are useful to us in the Forces of Light. You can walk among vampires without being suspected. Yet you are so young and your spirit still so transparent that you would be hard to trace with spells and wizardry if something should go wrong.

"We need you to enter the dwelling place of vampires. We need you to take within an object that I will find for you at great cost and deliver to you. You will take this object, enter the vampires' enclave, and find the small gate they have opened to Tch'muchgar's prison world. You will take the object through the gate, activate the object, and leave it there. Once activated, it cannot be moved or touched by anyone who is wicked or evil. It was very well designed at much expense."

"What is it?"

"It is called the Arm of Moriator."

"So you would like me to travel to another world, carrying a body part?" I say.

"No. You've misunderstood me. Arm as in arms race. It's an archaic usage. The Arm is in fact a magic disk a few inches wide. I think it's blue."

"What will it do?"

"I will explain precisely when the time comes, which will be in a few weeks. Let us say for the time being that the Arm of Moriator will stop Tch'muchgar from escaping when the vampires interrupt your townspeople's spells of binding. If he tries to escape from his prison world, he will pass out of that world but will not enter into another. He will thus cease to exist."

The celestial being winds his fingers together with a sense of finality. "Christopher, I am giving you the chance to save your world. I don't understand why you're standing looking confused and frightened. I am also giving you the chance to prove that you are, deep down, a human and not a vampire. If you can prove that to us, we will lift this curse. Your fate is tied up with this quest, Christopher. You can be a hero and a human. Or you can be a vampire. And degenerate. And be hounded down by a mob after you've chewed through the throat of some pretty girl in an alley."

I think about that, looking out across the reservoir. Tom and Jerk are sitting much farther down the bank, throwing stones into the water. Tom points across to one of the islands. I look there and see a large bird flapping among the trees. I say, "But I'm just—look, I'm—"

"Christopher, Christopher, your life depends on this. The lives of everyone you know, too. Remember, in four months you'll be ready for blood, unless you help. Remember the stake. Think about the squealing of your own vampiric little heart." He smiles. "I'll be in touch."

"What if I . . . ? Isn't there some other way?"

"There isn't. You won't be in danger. You're on the

cusp, remember? So you'll slip in and slip out. Un-detectable. I'm sorry I have to ask you to do this. It really won't be as difficult as it sounds. An adventure. Just give me a few weeks to retrieve the Arm of Moriator and then we'll talk. Three weeks is a long time when you're becoming a vampire."

My head is spinning. "I don't know," I say weakly. "I'll think about it."

"Christopher, this is the only way. Say yes."

For a minute I stand there looking at him frowning with his lips pressed together. A little girl is riding a bicycle with training wheels on the ridge above us. Her father chases her and calls, "Go, Stacey! Go!" He runs against the thickening clouds.

"Okay," I say. "If it's got to be."

"It has got to be. Is that a yes?"

"That's a yes. I'll help."

The celestial being laughs and claps once. "That's wonderful. You've made the right decision."

"I hope I have."

"You have. That's just great." He shakes his head. "This sure is a load off my mind. Now I can go and retrieve the Arm of Moriator for the next step."

"When will that be, again?"

"In about three weeks. I'll be in touch."

"Okay," I say. "What is your name?"

He looks surprised. "My name is nonverbal," he says. "It is a pattern of thought."

"You don't have a name?" I ask, somewhat incredulously.

"Okay, a name," he says, shrugging. "I don't know. Name . . . ? Chet."

"Chet?"

"That will do."

"Your name is Chet? Chet the Celestial Being?"

"Look," he says. "I don't need this."

"Do you really think I'm becoming a vampire?"

"You are becoming a vampire. Within a few months, you'll be a killer." He moves to rise. "Damn," says Chet the Celestial Being. "I am unused to physical existence and my leg has fallen asleep."

I part ways with Chet. He shakes my hand and says he knows I'll be perfect for the job. He says wait a few weeks and I'll start to see his point of view.

"Otherwise, Tch'muchgar and the Forces of Darkness will devour us all."

Then he limps away, doing the hokeypokey with his sleepy left leg.

I run toward my friends through the long, dead grass. I want so badly to be with them and to talk about stupid, normal things like B movies and truck scenes. The grass is all around my waist, exhaling in the wind. I am running, and my friends are now faceless bodies far, far off along the shore.

● ◗ ☾

Jerk, Tom, and I are walking back toward the dam, silently. Tom will not forgive me. He will not even talk to me. The afternoon is getting chilly. There are more clouds now than sun. Some people who were picnicking on the banks are standing up and shaking the grass out of their blankets.

None of us says anything. It is better that way. I am picturing a scene in the future when Tom will drop by my garret to visit, when he is bored and married and has an itsy-bitsy little life. He will come by my garret and find me amidst clutter, listening to vibraphone music and papier-mâchéing pictures of apes and cosmetic supplies to my girlfriend's nude body. I will have told her, "Once I was a vampire and saved the world."

We pass between two small brick sheds. One says "Grady '74." We do not speak. Tom is walking ahead of us. He chooses which path to follow back to the dam.

We walk down beside the cataract. The water splatters on boulders and struts.

Jerk asks me, "In *The Hitcher*, did you see that scene where the guy finds the finger in his french fries?"

"No, Jerk," I answer. "In the version I saw, they cut out just that scene."

My hunger grows. At dinner, I ask for my steak rare, and my brother calls me a bloodsucker. I try to change the subject. He keeps calling me a bloodsucker. My father is silent throughout the whole meal, except once, and that is because he likes a lot of butter on his potatoes.

I dream that night of killing Tom.

I dream we are in a fight. He says that something is not blue, and I say that it is green. So we fight, and I kill him and drink his warm blood; and as I do, I go from strength to strength. Then I realize that I am going to dream about Rebecca and am horrified. I will not let that happen. I wake up.

My sheets are twisted like a winding-sheet. It is black in my room, but I can see.

I do not feel like going to sleep. I am frightened. I am thirsty.

I pad down to the bathroom. I drink water and more water out of the faucet.

I turn it on warm. I want to drink the water warm. I gulp and gulp, but am not satisfied. It runs down my face and soaks the flannel collar of my pajamas.

I straighten up. I look in the mirror, and I see what I saw in the water earlier when I tackled Tom.

I have no reflection.

I pace in my room.

I am thirsty.

**CHAPTER 3** In the next few weeks there is spring rain. It rains all the time, rain like little spit pellets of dirty newsprint, tapping and gumming on windows and roofs. Out in the gray rain, there are sludgy buds hanging on the trees like chrysalises.

On the few days when the sun comes out, there's a dog-dung smell clogging the streets of town. For the people who live near cow fields, there's a cow-dung smell. In fact, our town is a kind of dung-smell smorgasbord.

People talk about the beauty of the spring, but I can't see it. The trees are brown and bare, slimy with rain. Some are crawling with new purple hairs. And the buds are bulging like tumorous acne, and I can tell that something wet, and soft, and cold, and misshapen is about to be born.

And I am turning into a vampire.

I receive the first vampire letter about four days after my discussion with Chet the Celestial Being.

It is on a cream card bordered in black. It says:

*The Children of the Melancholy One*
*cordially invite you*
*to a Gorging in the Shadows*
*every Thursday night*
*during the months of April, May, and June*

*Dress: Semiformal*                                       *11:00 P.M.*
*R.S.V.P. P.O. Box 165, Bradley*                       *drinks at 12:00*

On the back, in fountain pen, someone has written, "Christopher! We'd love to see you! We'll provide transport—just R.S.V.P. and we'll set up a car pool! Hope you can make it."

I have read it through three times when the writing fades and the paper withers to fine onionskin.

So they have found me. I ball up the letter to throw it away. This I mean to be a big gesture, showing that I will have none of them, but unfortunately the paper is so spiderweb thin and spongy by this time that I don't get that sense of rattle and crinkle that makes balling something up and throwing it away a really big event.

I am anxious because I don't know what to do. Obviously Chet the Celestial Being wants me to act with these inhumans as if I were happy to become one of them. Otherwise, I won't be able to slip in with Chet's magic Arm. But there is no way that I am going to visit vampires alone. There is no way that I am going to pencil in on my social calendar a gruesome kegger of death.

So I don't know what to do, and I wish he'd come back and tell me.

I wonder how he expects me to just figure things out with nothing to go on. I've never fought with the Forces of Darkness before. That was a Cub Scout badge I seem to have missed.

In the nights, I cannot sleep. I lie in my bed, and I hear the rain drumming and drumming until the roof must be numb.

I can hear others moving about the hallways, and sometimes I can hear them in sleep. I lie awake on my bed and I can hear them all, almost down to their pulse.

I can hear my mother snoring. I can hear my father turn uneasily. And after my brother thinks we are all asleep, I can hear him get his secret magazines from where they're hidden under his video equipment and use them.

But the worst is when I can hear no one. When there is no tread on the carpet in the hall, and I know I am alone.

When I was very small, there seemed to be a forbidden time after my parents went to sleep. It was fine when I lay awake and heard my parents talking softly down in the kitchen, or guffawing at sitcoms on the television.

But after they went to bed, and the dishwasher stopped running and sighed, and the house was silent, it seemed like I had found a vast abandoned lot of night where no one was allowed, and I was staggering in that place alone, with walls that held me from all who slept.

Now I feel that again because I can't sleep, and the same thoughts run again and again in my head.

I lie on my pillow one way, and when my cheek gets used to it, I turn the other way. I cannot sleep, and I think about that.

It is then that my thirst starts, in the dead hours.

I think: *I am so thirsty. I wish I could go to sleep. If I don't go to sleep, I will be sleepy tomorrow. I would sleep if I weren't so thirsty.* And these thoughts go on and on wheeling in circles and I get more and more desperate for something to break the silence.

Sometimes I get up and stare out the window. I stare out across the little lawn to the fence and then each moon-defined object there in the next yard: the plastic wading pool; the sun-bleached Big Wheel; the tangled apple tree.

And then I lift my eyes above the houses, above the comfortable roofs, and see the woods on the hills. And I sense then, in the way the moon drapes itself easily, obscenely over them all, that there is something wicked all around us, something staining the aluminum siding and the four-door sedans. There is something hiding behind it all, Tch'muchgar scheming, locked in darkness, and I pray to Chet the Celestial Being in my mind, if he can hear me, that he comes quickly so I no longer feel this danger in myself and out there on the hills.

And I lie in bed, turning this way and that. I think about how I got the curse. And when Chet will come. And what I should do.

Sometimes I can't stand the thirst and go to the bathroom and have a glass of water. But the water is too thin. I scoop it into my mouth, suck hard as I can, but I can't take in enough. I snap my teeth in midair. I clasp them and grind them and close my eyes. I want to hit something and feel flesh.

But I am standing still, my knees twitching in my pajamas. The thirst is upon me, so I am not in the mirror.

I sit on the bathroom floor, curled up in a ball. My arms are around my head as if someone were kicking me.

I can't wait to have burned out of me this stupid thirst, this hunger that lies coiled and miserable in my throat and stomach like a tapeworm.


After a wakeful night, I am thankful for my reflection in silverware. It's like silverware is what I've been waiting for all my life.

I walk downstairs and take real pride in the flash of my arm I see in the window in the front hall. I stop by the dining room table to check my face in the gloss of the table wax.

And I'm thankful for the little normal morning things my family says to one another. Like the way my father says, "I'm going to play golf with Dan this afternoon."

And the way my mother says, "Oh."

And the way my brother always pours a bowl of cereal for me really, really early so it gets soggy, then says in a voice like he's the patron saint of Fruity Pebbles, "Chris, look, I already poured a bowl of cereal for you."

Then I say, "This is all mush."

And my mother says, "Chris, your brother was doing you a favor making you breakfast. You are not going to throw away a perfectly good bowl of cereal just because you happen to be feeling finicky. Thank Paul. Sit down. Chew. Swallow."

I might argue, but I am so happy to see them all, and to see everything so normal, that I slurp up the mush and let it roll and slobber down my throat. "Mmmm! Mmm, mmm, mmm! Mmmm-*hmmmm*!" I exclaim, enjoying that wholesome American goodness.

I'm halfway through my bowl when I look down at my spoon. My reflection is still there. I'm obsessed with my reflection nowadays. I pick up the spoon and lick off all the milk.

My reflection stands out clearly, inverted. I turn from one side to the other. My nose swells and dances like the chorus line in a big Broadway Nose Revue. I move my head from one side to the other, and my nose kicks left, then right. One side, then the other. The nostrils are open so wide they must be belting out the finale from the end of act 3.

For a moment, I'm proud of my reflection. Then I look closer, and I'm not so happy. My hair is lanky and hangs down, from what I can see in the spoon. My eyes look sunken and dark and my features look haggard and ugly.

I hope nobody asks me why I look so tired.

My father and Paul get up from the table and leave.

I wonder whether anyone will notice how bad I look. People might start to guess why I haven't been sleeping well. They might start to notice before Chet comes back from his mysterious Arm errand and cures me of my curse.

"Chris," says my mother. "Earth to Chris."

I will have to wait to really talk to Rebecca Schwartz until Chet has healed me. I can't talk to her right now when it would be like a greasy lizard monster shambling up to her. I'll wait until after I'm back to normal, and sleeping. Then I'll buy some new clothes, too.

My mother is leaning against the table, looking at me with interest. "What do you think about when you start daydreaming like that?" she asks me. "You daydream all the time."

"Sorry," I say and put down the spoon.

"I really worry about you, Chris. Sometimes you are a complete space case. Someday you're going to have to stop daydreaming and do something," she says.

"Hey," I grumble. "I was just looking at the spoon."

"What?"

"I was just looking at a spoon. Okay? Looking at the flatware. That was all. Any other questions about me looking at the flatware?"

She shrugs and tosses out her coffee in the sink. She has a scowl on her face. "You're beyond me. You really are beyond me. I hope your father manages to understand you someday, because you really make no sense to me."

I don't mind that she says this. At least everything is normal, and there it is, my ugly reflection in my spoon.

I catch myself in the mirror when I go to the bathroom after breakfast. There is my uneven hair and my pasty face, and I don't even know if it's as ugly as sin or as beautiful as a reward for deeds well done.


After three sleepless nights in a row, it really starts to show. I lie there at night worrying because I'll be so bashed-up looking and stupid at school the next day. And in fact I am bashed-up looking and stupid at school. I'm sleepy and I can hardly eat. I sit there at lunchtime, hunched over my black cracked Fenway Frank, wishing it were liquid. It's pasted to the inside of my mouth. I keep gagging on the pieces of ash. Tom is across from me, watching me. He sees that I'm not eating much anymore, that I have not eaten much for days. I think he wonders why.

I fail a test. I sit in class not taking notes while my

teachers lecture and write things with chalk. After a few minutes of staring into space, I focus on the blackboard and realize that all this geometry and these words have just appeared in the last few minutes without any meaning to me, as if they were a natural phenomenon like frost scrawls on a window.

Tom hardly talks to me when we're at school now. I know the only way I can win him back is to be wide awake. I have to be extra funny to keep his interest. He is starting to hang out with other kids at school, like Chuck O'Hara and Andy Green. He hangs out with Jerk and me after school still, because he doesn't know the others well enough yet. Yet.

I want to tell him about Chet the Celestial Being, about my vampirism, and about the Vampire Lord in the lake. But I can't, not yet.

He still hasn't forgiven me for getting his lower left leg in the mud at the reservoir. Every time I speak to him, especially at school, I can tell that that lower left leg is hovering there between us, always making him angry, accusing me like a vengeful dismembered piece of an Edgar Allan Poe ghost, dripping duckweed.

I don't want anyone to notice anything different about me—the sleepiness or how I'm starting to get cranky and a little afraid of mirrors. I have to just keep smiling, that's the thing. Keep smiling for another few weeks, until the curse is lifted. Keep smiling, I think, while my teeth are still square.

One day my father keeps looking at me nervously, as if he's about to say, "Son, you know you have three eyes and a horn on your head?" But he doesn't say anything.

Then I hear my mother talking to him. "It's getting embarrassing," says my mother. "Just go up and tell him. What is so . . . ?"

"It's a turning point, Jennifer," says my father.

"A turning point?" says my mother.

"It was just yesterday he was in diapers. That's all I'm saying."

"For his sake, Norm," says Mom.

My father comes trudging up the stairs. I can hear his footsteps on the powder blue carpet. He picks up the stack of science magazines and *National Geographic*s that are sitting three steps up. He brings them up and sees me.

"Hey, Chris," he says.

"Aloha, Father," I say.

He is looking at me with the three eyes/horn look again.

"Chris." In his hands he flexes the magazines first one way, then the other. "Your mother and I were just thinking."

"I hope it didn't disturb your daily routine much," I joke.

He laughs a very little. "It's about time you shaved,"

he says. He coaxes the magazines into the shape of a tube—first, one that is a science magazine tube, then backward, so it's a *National Geographic* tube. "You're getting a little, you know. A little." He points at his upper lip. "You're a late bloomer, I know," he says.

I reach up and feel, and it is a little bit mossy on my upper lip.

"I can show you how," he says. "In the bathroom."

"I was just going to go watch television," I say.

"Your mother really would prefer if you got this over with."

"Please!" my mother contributes from the bottom of the stairs.

My father walks to the bathroom door (down the hall, first door on the right) and opens it. He turns on the light. I follow him in. He closes the door.

We are crowded together in the bathroom, my father and I, surrounded by mirrors and the mylar wallpaper's loud-beaked cockatoos. There is silver bamboo all around us on the walls. It's a jungle in there.

"You'll find there's nothing much to this," he says. "Soon you'll be doing it every day." Brief nostalgic pause. "My son."

"Paul already shaves," I say. "It's like no big deal."

My father says in a very professional way, "I think it's probably better that you learn to use a safety razor. The electric razor doesn't give you as smooth a shave."

"No? Well, I want a smooth shave," I say.

He shows me how to put on the shaving cream and wets the razor with hot water for me.

My mother says from the other side of the door, as if she's concerned, "How's it going in there, Chris?"

"Just fine, Mom," I say. "I've just learned about the foam. All systems go."

"Now take the razor," my dad says, "and put it just under your nose. Very carefully."

His fingers grab just below my wrist and guide my hand down. "Okay, you can let go now," I say, slightly annoyed. He pulls away, and the razor slips just a fraction. I say, "Ow."

He's saying, "There, now you've cut yourself." But what I'm noticing is the obvious thing. I can smell the steely tang of my blood.

I dive to the floor. I cry, "Blood!" I can feel my thirst rising. In a few seconds, I won't be visible in the mirror.

"What's wrong?" Dad asks.

"I dropped the razor," I say. "Can I do this alone? I think I need to learn to do this alone."

"Why? This is just the first time. You're bound to cut yourself once the first time."

I rise up halfway and start pushing him to the door, but I'm hunched over, below the level of the counter. "Get out," I whine. "Could you get out, Dad? I want to do this alone."

"Hey, okay, okay," he says, backing out. "What's the problem?"

"I'd rather do this myself," I say. "That's enough bonding for now."

He steps out and I slam the door behind him and press the lock in with my thumb.

When I am alone, I recite five times, "Shit shit shit shit shit."

I step over to the mirror, where of course my reflection no longer appears.

"What's the matter with him?" my mother asks.

"I don't know," my father answers, sounding weary. "It was only a little cut."

I consider what to do. My face is slithering with shaving cream. But not in the mirror. The foam is dropping on my shirt. I hold up my hand right next to the mirror and press it against the cool glass. It leaves a baby's breath trace of mist. Otherwise, nothing.

I'll have to fly this thing blind. It's like one of those airplane disaster movies.

"Just remember," my father is saying through the door, "up and down, but never sideways."

"Are you okay, Chris?" my mother pleads.

"What's his problem?" I hear Paul ask.

My hand is shaking; I raise my razor to my face again. I am surrounded by the accusatory stares of the wall cockatoos.

Carefully, I drag the razor down my lip again.

I touch it with my finger.

More red. I start licking. The shaving cream is not as

sweet as it smells. The blood is good and salty. There isn't much from just two wounds.

So I take another couple of exploratory scrapes with the razor. Without the mirror this is just a joke. I am cutting the hell out of my face.

And I'm loving it. I'm licking and licking like I am one big happy Fudgsicle; and pretty soon, I'm laughing, and the jazzy cockatoos and cockatrices are laughing with me.

Mom and Dad and Paul are still calling in to me, "Chris, are you okay?" "Chris, is it going all right?" "Hey, Chris, you done? I gotta whizz." But I can barely contain myself. I've dropped the razor in the sink, and I'm standing there, as light as invisibility, and licking, and laughing, and licking.

I laugh and laugh.

"This is . . . I mean! Oh! Can you . . . ?" I hoot, and no one understands.


I need to wait for the bleeding to die down before I can unlock the door. I have to wait for the blood to clot.

"What's taking you so long, Chris?" asks my mother.

Paul snorts, "Like it's shaving he's doing for the first time in there."

"Paul!" says my mother. "You apologize to Chris! When he comes out."

When the blood clots, which is quickly, and I reappear, I have a couple of small triangular cuts that don't amount to much. I have three thin red lines on my upper lip, like a mustache drawn with a ruler in red pen.

That is the story of my first shave.

The day after my first shave Rebecca Schwartz and I talk. I am feeling very sleepy because I didn't sleep much the night before.

She says, "Oh, Chris, what happened to your face?"

I instinctively flip my tongue up to feel the three crusted lines.

I shrug and look at the metal leg of a desk. "I, you know. I had this shaving accident," I say.

She winces. "Looks like it hurt," she says.

"Yeah," I say. We stare at each other.

She suggests, "Next time leave the rototiller outside."

Then someone calls for her, and she excuses herself and walks away.

She floats above the tiles, wearing a Laura Ashley dress. At least, I think it's a Laura Ashley dress. I mean, I haven't gone up behind her and flipped the tag or anything.

A few seconds later, I think what I should have said was "Lion taming."

Damn.

Then, in gym I am doing pushups, and suddenly I

realize I could have said, "It was a duel. Sabers. You know, defending your honor."

Then she'd say slyly, "Oh, yes, Tom told me you get very fierce when my honor's at stake."

And I'd say, "Of course. It was at dawn out back of the A&P."

And she'd laugh, and I'd see something in her eyes.

That is not what happened.

Instead I was sleepy and said shaving wound.

The shaving wound was not as good a story.

For instance, there's no part about romance and a shaving wound in all of *The Three Musketeers* or *The Count of Monte Cristo*.


There are more vampiric murders in the news that week The most brutal is in Northborough. Two victims are found together. They are a boy and a girl, caught fooling around in the woods. It is established that the vampire drank the boy first, in front of the girl. She evidently tried to run away, but her pants were around her ankles, so she could only waddle about fifteen feet before the vampire walked up behind her.

They are found in the morning. The vampire is not found at all.


The way they eat disgusts me.

We are in our family dining room, which is part of the kitchen and separated by a counter. My parents had track lighting installed in the kitchen, so we can turn off the light near the refrigerator and stove and have only lights from above shine on the table. In spite of the fact that we have nothing to say to one another, my parents insist that we should eat together because we are a family. We each think things alone, and occasionally say things that might be of interest to one another.

E.g., "These peas are a bit overcooked."

And, "Stop complaining. Your father and I worked hard to put this dinner on the table."

And, "I wasn't complaining. I was just developing my critical faculties."

And, "Do you want to develop your critical faculties with a TV tray in the garage?"

But the main thing is the chewing. That I see now.

I cannot believe how loud human ingestion is. I sit there, unable to eat, astonished. I am staring at my plate with eyes as big as plates. I can't believe my ears, hearing the factoryful of noises, the squelching and popping, crunching and scratching. The rattle of forks against ceramic. The slurp of liquids. The clanging of glasses against teeth.

It's like cannon fire. It's like hydraulic tubes and stormy surf against bleak rocky islands.

They sit there, unaware of how grotesque their feeding is. They're hunched below the clean strip lights like praying mantises—and I sit horrified as they cut burned legs and chests apart, and feed them into their greedy mandibles, and smile like nothing's wrong.

"Eat, Chris," says my mother. "You don't think I cook for my own good, do you?"

My father looks at me over his glasses. He chews three times with a sound like the Swamp Thing learning how to use crutches. What he says is "Come on, Chris. You need to put a little flesh onto those bones."

At 11:53 P.M., about two weeks after I speak to Chet the Celestial Being, an evil mouth appears on TV. At that time all television reception in Clayton and Bradley and all the surrounding towns suddenly fails. There is nothing but static for a second. I am upstairs lying in bed already, but I hear my father swear downstairs.

The next day, it's on the local news. They play tapes of what came on.

The static, a gray sludge spanking again and again across the screen, spits and jabs out a messy outline—a huge maw—crooked teeth like mountains gagging and croaking—and a voice, growling and gutteral, howls through the raging storm of static:

*. . . out . . .*
*. . . trapped and . . .*
*. . . you maggots little maggots . . .*
*Release—! . . . this torment! Torment! Our hatred—*

*Soon! . . . Now! Trapped!*
*Your blood, damn you, all you . . .*
*. . . out of this place . . .*

Then there is a wailing that is so ferocious and yet so melancholy that it blasts the regularly scheduled programs back on TV.

Nobody knows where the transmission came from. The rest of the night on television is as placid as a cold mountain pool that nobody has found or stirred.

There is not a hint of what dark god must struggle somewhere, writhing back and forth to escape.

The second vampire letter I get is from a girl, the morning after there was a mouth on TV. Paul can tell the letter is from a girl because of the handwriting and he steals it and runs around the room with it singing, "Chris has got a girl! Chris has got a girl!"

"Give it back," I demand. "Give me back my letter!"

He makes a wimp face and mewls, "Give me back my wedder! Give me back my wedder!"

"Give it!"

"Give it, pwease, big bwudder! Give it back to me, pwease, my widdle wedder!"

"Don't ever change, Paul. I hope you always keep this boyish charm."

"Paul," says my mother sharply. "Give him the letter. It's his. Okay?"

So he gives it back.

I read it alone in my room. It is written on ruled notebook paper in purple felt tip pen. Some words, the special ones, are in all different colors. It is from a girl named Lolli Chasuble.

It says:

*Dear Christopher,*

*How R U? You don't know me, but I know you! My father asked me to write a letter. So here it is! One of my friends saw you in Bradley a few weeks ago, and we were hoping you'd come and get to know some of us. We're really very nice, and you have nothing to lose. What are we going to do?—bite your head off? (joke! ☺)*

*No, seriously! I know you must be scared. I was too!!! The first time my dad told me I had to drink blood, I was totally grossed out. But now I'm like, "Shit, this is great!" and, "Is there a diet variety?"*

*People say lots of dumb shit about vampires that isn't really true. My dad says you're a pretty brainy guy, so I guess I don't need to tell you that we don't have to wear stupid black capes like in flicks or live in big smell-o-rific castles. I just dress in cool normal clothes, meaning bike shorts, a T-shirt, etc., etc.*

*Being one of us is cool because you're always on the move, like I've lived most of my life in Los Angeles, which I L-O-V-E-D* [that word is in different color felt tips]*, but I've also lived all over the West Coast, since my father had to run away from L.A. It's pretty tough sometimes not having a real address — I have to get my monthly issue* of Sassy at the newsstand! But there are some of us in every city. We have G-R-E-A-T parties ☺ and do all sorts of cool secret stuff!

We also have more fun than mortals, who are just waiting around to die. For one thing, the night is ours, and for another thing, if you've heard of French kissing, we have something called Transylvanian kissing, which is when we bite each other's tongue and exchange blood. Omigod, it is totally sexy! With mortals, sometimes it's fun to make out with them before you kill them—go, girl!

Anyway, I hope you'll come to meet us soon. I'd really like to meet you! The thing is, if you don't come to us soon and learn the ropes from my dad and his friends, you'll probably freak way out in a couple of months or so and get hunted down and killed.

God, not to part on a morbid note! So, I'm looking forward to seeing you! OK?

Luv ya,


Lolli Chasuble


P.S. I don't have a boyfriend right now. There was this guy I had a total crush on at school—he was a complete H-U-N-K-O-R-A-M-A—did I want to get inside his shorts! And he would have been mine, too, except that after the car crash his parents had him C-R-E-M-A-T-E-D! ☹ Oh, well! Say la vie!

P.P.S. My father says you were in CCD or Sunday school or something for a while. Yawnsburg Central, U.S.A.! Make sure you don't bring any crosses or anything to the meeting, because we worship an eternal being called Tch'muchgar who shall soon lead us to victory.

P.P.P.S. My address is P.O. Box 163 in Bradley, MA, 08545. Write!

That is my letter from Lolli Chasuble.

I fold it up and plan to keep it. Then I realize Paul might search my room for it, so instead I tear it up into a thousand pieces and throw them away. I chew on some of them first so he won't try to put it back together.

I don't know what Chet would want me to do. I have heard nothing from him. He is due in another week.

The next day I see a scene that convinces me that it makes real sense for me to have a crush on Rebecca Schwartz. I go into the library to sit hidden in the back aisles, furtively flipping through a book entitled *The Undead: Famous Real-Life Vampires*. As it happens, Rebecca is sitting at a table nearby. She is drawing idle dandelions on a notepad, reading books entitled things like *The Cabala: Ancient Route to Power* and *The Lost Spells and Incantations of Hermes Trismagistus*.

Through the wide sixties windows a gray light falls. The panes are smeared with the dull newsprint rain, and down on the street I can see cars stopping monotonously at the stoplight and waiting to go. Inside, the gray light shows up small dirty details of people's faces, like the grease in the creases of chins, and the mangy stubble on upper lips, and the limp hair, hanging like dead weeds on their heads. The stains and wrinkles on their clothes.

All but Rebecca Schwartz. The light sets her face in

the matte perfection of porcelain, and she seems, even more, to be poised in the midst of monsters.

"Hi," I say.

She says, "Hi," and slips her eyes back down to the book.

"Too bad about the rain," I say.

She looks up for a moment. "It's good for the flowers," she says.

I nod. She looks down. So I turn my back to her and crouch against the bookshelf and start flipping through the vampire book for parts I haven't read yet.

We both read for a while. I am reading a detailed account of the life of Vlad the Impaler and she is reading *The White Arts: An Introduction* when Kristen Mosley walks over to Rebecca's table. Rebecca notices her coming. I'm interested to see Rebecca smoothly shuffle some school papers over her books, those strange books of power.

"Hi," says Kristen to Rebecca. "I've been thinking: Does history make, like, any sense at all?" This is quite an impressive question and one that might take a long time to answer, but Kristen continues, "God, this rain is, like, driving me crazy. It is making everything so wet. It's hopeless. Can you do this history thing at all? I think it makes no sense. What are you *reading*?"

Rebecca looks startled. She shifts her papers to the side. "These?" she says. "These were here when I sat down."

"Were you *reading* them?"

Rebecca squirms. "They're sort of interesting. They're about ancient magic."

Kristen listens. She fixes Rebecca with a look that says, *Okay. Now even my jaw is bored with you.* Then she says, "Yeah. Whatever. Are you gonna come over and do the history with us, or what? The guys are like, 'Where's Rebecca? We need someone with, like, an actual *brain* at our table.'" The two of them laugh.

"Okay," says Rebecca brightly, leaving her stack of books. "I'm there!"

She looks at me as she turns away—over Kristen's shoulder—and suddenly I know that there is a price to her popularity. There is a silent pact between her and Kristen, one which I have witnessed and am expected not to mention. Kristen will not tell anyone that Rebecca reads strange, boring books, as long as Rebecca agrees not to talk about them and embarrass them both. She has her secret interests, too; and she doesn't care that I know. She thinks I will keep her secret.

This makes me feel a little better.

I put the book about famous vampires back on the shelf and head out into the afternoon rain to kick pebbles on the street. I'm feeling so happy that kicking pebbles in the rain could be a wacky, hip solo on the jazz saxophone.

It's that kind of game.

● ◑ ☾

Sometimes late at night I think about Rebecca when I can't get to sleep.

I can't ever really get to sleep.

I think about if we were the last two people on earth, because I've made her into a vampire, which is very romantic, and we've withstood the radioactivity and all the madness of nuclear war. Outside, the ancient crumbling city is razed beneath the blood-red sunset moon.

We lie together in a room at the top of a tall, tall stone tower, far in the air. We lie side by side, draped in silk that slithers between her legs, and we feel the pressure of each other's bodies while outside, huge mutant bats beat against the walls.

One night I am watching the news with my mother. She has an afghan over her lap.

On the news, a woman is being tried for manslaughter. She thought that the faeries had snatched away her twin babies and put elfin changelings in their place. You are supposed to throw changelings in the fire after you say prayers and chants. She did that. She threw the twins in the fire. She was right about one: it was a changeling and scurried up the chimney, stretching like a mantis, wheezing and whining. The other was not a changeling. It burned.

My mother, watching, holds her hand to her mouth so the fingers are limp and touch the top lip. She says, "I can't believe it. I can't believe she'd throw her baby on the fire."

"There were two," I point out. "Two babies."

"One of them wasn't even hers," my mother says. "It wasn't even human."

*It wasn't even human.* I get up and go into the den. I sit there, looking out the window for a minute. What would she do, my mother, if she found out a son of hers was not human? Then I go and get out the photo album. I look at photos of me when I was small. There I am, walking by the reservoir. I have made a Tinkertoy ray gun and have shot my mother as part of my plan to invade the earth. She is laughing and falling backward, clutching her heart. She is laughing so hard, and I'm laughing, too, holding my ray gun, invading her world.


I am walking to school through one of the abandoned mills. It's a shortcut from home. The parking lot is chipped and breaking out in stubbly dead grass.

The factory buildings loom over me like a canyon. Rows of empty, dark windows in abandoned sweatshop galleries hang above me in the sky. There are sagging slate roofs and broken glass and wide doors covered in plywood and nailed shut. On the brick wall someone has sprayed green words reading "Sheila loves Mike for a while." I walk between the buildings slowly, listening to the sound of my sneakers on the gravel.

One of these mills was closed after a big fire. There weren't enough exits, and fourteen women were trapped upstairs and burned to death. The rumor is that on some nights you can see them still, those fourteen women, shrieking as they work at flaming looms, producing strange garments for an inhuman overseer. It's a desolate place.

Suddenly I hear something.

Footsteps.

Who would be here at this abandoned place at this hour of the morning?

I look up at the empty angles of the brick walls against the sky. I look the other way, across the broken pavement.

Someone is walking slowly, surely, toward me.

I don't know why, but this figure outlined against the sky frightens me. It is obviously staring at me. It is obviously coming right toward me. It walks mechanically, relentlessly.

That is when I start running.

I scamper up some concrete steps. I pivot on the rusty handrail and run off to the left between broken factory buildings. I throw myself down the alley. Only a few more turns and I'll be back out on a main street.

From around the corner, I can hear that the figure is gaining at an inhuman pace. It couldn't have gone up the steps with feet.

I burst out onto the street. Cars are whipping past.

Birds are shooting through hedges. A motorcycle revs.

I move away from the alley and up the road, glancing backward. I wait to see who's coming after me.

I stand there.

No one comes.

The unglassed windows of the factory are blackened with ancient soot, dark carbon licks of women who sewed petticoats. The walls face blankly on the street.

No one comes.

There is no sign that anyone was with me between the factories at all.

I continue cautiously on my way to school. I walk up the hill past the town green. Up a steep lane past the house of a man who owns sixteen old cars, all of them without wheels. By the time I reach the first of the streets in my school's neighborhood, I can tell that I'm being followed again.

The strange thing is that the man (for at first I assume it's a man) is not subtle at all. I have read about a billion spy novels, and when you are following someone, you hide behind newspapers, or pretend to paint the house next door, or hide a camera inside a spacious poodle.

You don't just walk calmly after your prey and stand across the street from him, right on the sidewalk, staring.

He is wearing a cheap baggy suit and a blue polyester

tie with raised paisleys. His face is wide and stern. His hair is in one piece, all pulled back and oiled into waves. That is how I first know that he is not of this earth. No human would willingly have that hair.

His eyes do not blink or move. He does not look like he is comfortable in his body.

He follows me to school. He waits on the circle at the base of the American flag, and every class I'm in he turns like the shadow on a sundial to face the windows.

He follows me home. I am petrified. In my house, I cling to rooms where people are sitting. My family starts looking at me strangely. I can see him through windows, standing across the street, staring.

He stands there through the afternoon. No one else has noticed him.

He stands there as night falls.

During dinner, he treads right up to the window, peering. I scream and back away from the table. His face is inches from the glass. His eyes are dead. He is staring at me.

Everyone else looks around the kitchen and asks me what's wrong.

When I look out, he is back across the street, staring at us.

I ask Paul if I can sleep in his room. He says not until I fix my little bed-wetting problem, ha ha ha.

It must be some kind of supernatural servant of Tch'muchgar. That is all I can think. It must be a spirit like Chet, but working for evil instead of good. It is watching to see whether I will respond to the vampires' letters, or whether I will just be a danger to them. It wants to see whether I go out at night, and range through the town, and find my gory prey. It stands there, just biding its time.

That night, when I can't sleep, I can feel the Thing with the One-Piece Hair staring in at me. I can feel its line of sight shooting through the window, ricocheting off the lamp, and striking me.

I get up at about three and peek out the window.

There are a few streetlights. It is standing near one of them. Its arms are at its sides.

Its dead eyes stare at me still.

They are staring, and it waits.

Paul and I are watching the double funeral for the two teenage lovers killed in Northborough by vampires.

The national tabloids have made the story into a big morality issue as a warning to teens and hysterical parents. Their headlines are things like "NO NECKING!" WARNS NORTHBOROUGH'S NAPE-NIBBLING NOSFERATU. The funeral is on the Catholic channel during prime time.

Paul says, "I can't believe these media buttscoops. You know, who are the real vampires here?"

I am crouched down to watch the show because the

Thing with the One-Piece Hair is standing with its face pressed to the window. Its nose leaves no grease on the pane.

I am terrified, curled up into a ball so it can't see me behind the plaid sofa. But I know it is still standing there. My parents are out, and I don't want to be in a room without my brother.

"Are you okay?" Paul asks.

"I have a stomachache," I say.

"You've been sick a lot lately," he says.

After the commercial break, the show moves on to the psalms.

"I can't believe they're doing this close camera work on these people. The mother and sisters are, like, bawling their eyes out and the camera's loving it," says Paul.

On the screen, the father of the girl, voice cracking like a kid's, is intoning one of the Bible readings. "In the mountains, there is a voice of mourning, crying, and wailing; it is Rachel, who weeps for her children, and will not be comforted, for they are no more."

His voice floats through the dark forests, past the blinking radio towers on lonely hills; it floats past the empty squares and pizza joints with buzzing signs, and into the neat white houses by the green, into the shacks down near the old factories.

And everywhere at once, he lowers his head; and everywhere at once, his voice falls silent.

# CHAPTER 4

One night, Tom and Jerk decide to go on a vampire hunt.

I do not think it is a very good idea. I say I don't generally seek the company of anything with fangs. There are three of us, however, which always means that it's one against two. I end up protesting uselessly. Tom has not quite forgiven me for trying to beat him up, so I have to play along.

I really don't want to go at all. The Thing has been following me off and on for three days, and I don't want to go out of the house more than is absolutely necessary. But I have to. Tom has started watching me at school. He can see that I have not been sleeping well. He notices at lunch that I am not eating well. I am worried that he might have guessed what is wrong. Maybe it is nothing; but maybe he knows.

He is judging me carefully. There's a suspicion in the way he looks at me. I can tell that this vampire hunt idea of his is a test. He has something up his sleeve.

I am terrified that he might know. And once he knows for sure, he will blow the whistle.

I do not have much homework, and I do it all before dinner. I have to translate a dialogue between two French people buying greeting cards. After dinner, I lie to my mother.

"I'm going over to play video games with Tom and Jerk," I say.

"Video games?"

"At Tom's house," I say. "His mother said it was okay."

"Get your father to drive you. I don't want you walking after dark."

"Why?"

"You know why."

"It's only about five minutes to Tom's house."

"I don't want you walking after dark."

"At all?" I say. "Can I crawl?"

"Don't get sarcastic with me, Chris. I said I don't want—," and so on. We have this sort of conversation for a while. In the end, my father drives me.

While we drive over to Tom's, which is about a minute's drive, my father listens to the oldies station and hums along. Occasionally he'll remember three words and sing them. The blossoms are coming out on some of the trees. The telephone lines are drooping over the street.

It's about half an hour later that we set out for the forest. Tom's parents know we are going, but they are lax and not very bright. "Have a good time!" they say. "Be careful!"

We pick up Jerk on the way. The two of them insist on bringing Jerk's dog, Bongo.

Bongo runs around the three of us, huffing. He

bounces on me for a while. Then he bounces on Tom.

"We are not taking that dog," I say.

"Why?" says Jerk. "If he'd like to he can come."

"Who says?" I ask.

"Let him bring the dog," says Tom, who is being bounced on. Tom bumps his palms against Bongo's chest to fend the animal off. "It'll protect us," he says

"That stupid dog will no more protect us—"

"He is not stupid," says Jerk hotly.

"He is stupid."

"He is not stupid."

"Jerk," I say, "that dog is stupider than a thing made out of wood."

But Tom is being indulgent with Jerk, so he says that Jerk can bring the dog if he wants and what is my problem. We head off for the town forest.

It is dark by now. The stars are only out sometimes, as clouds keep sliding in front of them. The trees are scratching in the breeze.

We go through a few streets of houses. Most of the town is old, tall houses, or at least the memorable part is. The part where Jerk lives is all short and squat, and it's looking a little rundown. A few windows are lit badly and dimly, like aquarium lights.

We kick a stone back and forth, and I lose it in a drain.

"How long do we have to hunt for vampires?" I ask Tom. "When do we give up?"

"You don't have to come," says Tom sourly. He perches his eyebrows carefully, as if he's studying me, speculating.

I shrug. "I just want to know when we're going to turn around."

"What's your problem tonight?" he says.

We go under the metal railroad bridge. On the brown iron panels, someone has spray painted "Goat legs."

The road winds up the hillside, and for the moment we stick to it, as it is very dark out.

Tom and Jerk are now walking side by side in front of me.

My thoughts are wandering, and Tom and Jerk are heading off into the woods. We step over branches.

Jerk has finally caught up to the debate of twenty minutes ago. He suddenly adds, "And plus, Bongo will be able to detect vampires."

"Come on," I say.

"When dogs see something supernatural their hackles go up."

"What? What is a hackle?" I demand. "I don't know if I want to see your dog with its hackles going up."

Tom has brought along a flashlight, and now he takes it out of his coat pocket. He starts shining it around the trees.

"Did you see last year when they were in Montana?" he asks.

"The vampires?" says Jerk.

"Yes, in Montana," Tom affirms. "They had on the news—"

"I remember that," says Jerk. He wheels his arm to push aside a springy branch. I am still behind them, so I catch it as it snaps back.

"Did you see the footage?" asks Tom. "There were farmers—they showed pictures—farmers who were caught by vampires. They showed these pictures of these farm machines with these corpses sitting in them, and their heads were all just blood and this pulpy substance, and their clothes were all stained."

"Then," I suggest, "it is somewhat curious that I find myself looking for vampires."

"Chris is complaining again," Tom says to Jerk.

Jerk says that Tom could cut me some slack.

"I'm not complaining," I say. "I'm just—" But I can't think of what to say, so I squint up between the boughs and I don't say anything.

We are climbing up the hill now. Down on the road I can hear someone honking a horn. They honk it twice. Maybe they saw someone they knew, or maybe once just wasn't enough.

The dead trees are all around us, and the slope is increasing. The circle from Tom's flashlight wobbles ahead of the two of them. Their silhouettes block the light. Bongo skitters between them. They are talking quietly. I feel very alone in back of them, in the darkness, while they walk together with their secret jokes. I keep picturing white fingers closing on my shoulders.

In a few minutes, the hill gets steeper. The trees on the summit are low and barren. The water tower hangs above us on its daddy longlegs.

Through the twisted trees we can see down into the valley. We can see the lights of the town center and the black waters of the reservoir. On three distant hills, three radio towers wink, gently soaking the valley in silent soft rock.

I turn from the view and see that Tom and Jerk are looking expectantly around, as if they actually thought they'd see a vampire on the bare hilltop. It is not the worst place to catch a vampire. The trees are so low and brittle and the sky so close that it looks like a devil's orchard.

"Here we are," I say. "I guess we just came on the wrong night. Can we go?"

Tom narrows his eyes and says carefully, "What's the matter? Why are you so down on this?"

"Because it is stupid," I say. "What would you do if you met a vampire?" The wind picks up all around us. "You know, vampires have the strength of ten men."

"Ten?" says Tom.

I shrug. "It was an estimate."

"Which ten?"

"I said it was an estimate."

The pale trees are shivering.

"Oh, Jesus Christ, Tom," I say. "This is just stupid."

"If this is so stupid," says Tom pointedly, "why are you out here?"

I scramble for an answer. Tom is staring at me, shining the light in my eyes. I raise my hand to block the light out of my face. I wonder if he's looking at my mouth.

"Hm?" Tom prompts.

I gabble lamely, "I'm—I'm a victim of peer pressure."

"What?" says Jerk.

"Shut up," says Tom. He has turned and is walking away through the squat trees. He says, "We're sick of your complaining."

Now the wind is very violent on the hilltop. The dead branches are clacking together.

Tom and Jerk are running away from me. They are leaving me alone in the night.


I run to catch up with them, but I am too slow. They are hopping by strides through the trees.

I dash as quickly as I can through the creaking branches. The branches tear at me and I can't see well— my night vision has been blotted out by Tom's flashlight. I can hear them ahead of me, and Bongo I see a couple of times, flying one way or another.

I am completely alone now. That is what I realize.

Tom and Jerk must hate me. Even if Tom is just playing a stupid joke and does not realize how close he has come to the truth, to my secret, this trick, this dumb trick, shows he can't be trusted. Whatever happens to me, I can't tell them now.

I catch glimpses of light in front of me. I can't tell if it's the flashlight or the headlights of some car, prowling on the dark road below.

I stop and listen.

Everything is silent, except the wind in the trees. It rocks them gently.

Something scurries through the woods above me, back toward the hilltop. I think it is a falling branch or some other piece of forest detritus.

Now I can see the trunks of trees. My vision has improved. I can see the tree trunks standing.

I stand there in that groping wood. I try to get my bearings.

Pushing at the bracken, I head down toward the base of the hill.

There is someone behind me, stalking through the woods.

"Tom," I call. "Jerk."

But there is only one person, one pair of footsteps, and it has sped up now that it has heard my voice. There is no answer. Just a quick walking.

I turn; I run. I'm lost in a choking nest of firs. I keep brushing them out of the way. There are more.

The Thing with the One-Piece Hair. It must be the Thing.

I look behind me and see it pacing down the hill, chasing me. Branches rake across its dead flesh, but it doesn't push them out of the way. Some of them snap off against its face. It has its eyes locked on me and does not blink.

I am scrambling through underbrush, and sticks jam against my arms, and I am all alone in the echoing forest with the Thing.

It keeps walking toward me, with its arms hanging at its sides. I can hear it, and while I am hopping through the bracken and the broken trees, its steps are perfectly rhythmic.

"Help!" I am screaming as loud as I can. "God, will you help! Help! Help! Help! No!"

The ghastly emptiness of the forest, the miles and miles of hikeable trail, the lonely roads, no relief I can think of—

And then I hear its voice. It speaks not in one voice, but in the voice of a congregation, with the voices of women and men together, calling as one, "Stop. Do not run. That will mean more pain for you. Running will mean more pain. Stop."

I look back, and it is not far behind me, just the length of a bus, except that buses don't go through the woods; and it is stretching out its sluggish arm toward me—and it calls a strange word—

And as if in a dream, I cannot move except in slow motion. My foot rebounds against the ground—I push myself off and creep forward through the strangling air.

The Thing is walking closer.

I grab on to trees and try to pull myself along. "God!" I try to scream, but the air is as thick as Jell-O in my lungs. I feel it purging outward, slow and thick as phlegm. I am mute. I am trapped in an arc, both my feet off the ground.

The Thing steps over a tree trunk.

I feel the ripple as my heart beats once.

The Thing raises its hand. It looks for a moment at its blunt, dusty fingers. And then the monster's cold flesh wraps around my wrist.

Suddenly, time is real again.

I scream at the top of my lungs.

It looms its face in mine, like a bird studying its prey. Its mouth is frowning, and it does not breathe.

It whispers in the voice of a hundred hissing, "You are foolish for running. You will be heard, and things will be harder for you."

It stares at me, its dead face full of glazed anger.

"Now," it grunts.

It raises its hand, as if to strike. I cower.

"Back off from the boy," says Chet, who has walked into the clearing.

The Thing with the One-Piece Hair swivels its head to look at him

"He is mine," Chet the Celestial Being explains, his voice hard. "Get away from him. Get away. Step away."

The Thing releases me. Chet nods slowly.

The moon shines down into the clearing. The trees are old and elegant. For a moment, the three of us stand there and regard one another.

Then Chet the Celestial Being slams his hands together and a bolt of blue fire shoots out and blasts the Thing.

There are just the two of us then.

Chet's bolt has left behind not so much as a smoldering toupee.

"Come on," says Chet. "It will take him twenty minutes or so to rematerialize. By that time we want to be in my car, where he can't track you."

"You have a car?" I ask.

"Special issue," Chet explains, gesturing down the hill. We start to walk. "For the transfer of mortals. It's time we moved along to the next stage of the plan. I've spent the last few weeks retrieving the Arm of Moriator from where it was stored. We're going to the convocation of vampires. The heart of things. Now. No time to lose."

We run down across through the woods. We climb over a stone wall. The moon picks out each tanning lichen on the stone.

"What was that?" I ask. "That Thing?"

"What did it look like?" says Chet

"A servant of Tch'muchgar?" I guess. "You know, some demon?"

"Exactly."

"It's been watching me for days."

"Tch'muchgar probably wanted to see what you were up to."

"Then doesn't he know that I'm not on his—"

"Look, we don't have time to discuss this now," Chet chides, stopping in his tracks. "Do you want me to put a sign of protection on you?"

"What?"

"I can place my sign on you, my sigil, which will mark you and protect you so that the Thing you saw back there and others like it can never harm you. I can place the sigil on you now, which can never be removed. Would you like that?"

I am feeling a little nervous about all this. "Well," I say.

"I can do it right now." Chet lifts up my right arm. "I'll place the sign here." He turns over my wrist and touches a spot just below my watchband. "All right?"

I look up at his face. I feel nervous, like the blood is running out of my fingers and arms. I nod.

He closes his eyes and mutters to himself. When I look down, there is a red mark there, a red sunburst like a tiny tattoo.

He releases my arm, which swings down to my side. "There," he says. "You're protected. Marked. That beast we just saw can't touch you. No being like it can touch you. Satisfied?"

Once again, I look up at his face. My fingers are cold. I nod.

"Hurry up then. We have no time to lose." And he plunges off into the forest.

We come out on one of the roads. Chet has an infallible sense of direction. His car is right there, a black Cadillac, sitting dark on the shoulder of the road. I have heard of the black Cadillacs that travel about the country on strange errands.

"This is it," he says, his brogues clicking across the pavement.

I say, "I'm glad to see the Forces of Light drive American."

"It's a piece of junk," says Chet. "Late eighties. It doesn't even have antilock brakes. Is that your friends?"

It is. They're running out onto the road.

"Hey, Chris," bellows Jerk. "You okay?" He rubs his hand through his mossy hair.

They're walking over to us.

"I'm fine," I say.

I look nervously at Chet the Celestial Being, but he is keeping his celestial cool. He extends his hand and says, "Hi. I'm Chet, a friend of Christopher's parents. Nice to meet you."

"Horatio," says Tom, shaking Chet's hand.

"It's nice to meet you, Horatio," says Chet.

"I'm Michael," says Jerk. "But my friends call me Jerk."

"They . . . ? I see." Chet strides to the side of the car. "Well, it was very nice to meet you both. I was just about to drive Christopher home."

"Oh," says Jerk, delighted. "If it wouldn't be a real problem, could you, like, drop me back at home? Me and my dog?"

"No dogs allowed," says Chet. "This isn't my car."

"Okay," says Jerk; but Tom intervenes.

Tom says, "We'll be right on the way. There won't be time for the dog to shed."

"No, sorry," says Chet. "Nothing that creepeth upon four feet. That counts out the dog."

"And you, Jerk," Tom adds.

"Ha ha ha," says Jerk.

I say uneasily, "If it would be possible . . . Chet . . . maybe we should take them home. I'm just worried about that strange . . . man we saw? That he might still be around?"

Chet frowns for an instant. "I don't think these two need to worry about him."

I say quietly, "It would make me feel better."

"All right," says Chet.

"Which man?" Tom asks.

That's how we all end up in Chet's car. Tom, Jerk, and Bongo are in the back seat. I'm in the passenger seat. I can tell Chet is mad. He starts the car, gives me a look that shows he is irritated but getting over it, and heads down the road.

We wind through the forest for a few minutes. It doesn't help that Tom is trying to embarrass me in front of my parents' supposed friend by lying as boldly as possible. "So my mother says to me, 'Horatio, I don't want you walking around at night, Horatio. Is that understood, Horatio?'", etc., etc.

"Horatio," says Chet, "I wonder if you could be quiet for just a quick moment while I think."

So Tom grins at Jerk in the back seat and winks. Jerk is embarrassed. After a few minutes, Tom gets bored; so he starts to play with the electric windows.

"Window race!" he calls, and he and Jerk each try to be the first one to put his window down.

"Would you cut that out?" says Chet.

"Window race!" Tom calls again.

"Would you—?"

"Mine won't go up anymore," says Jerk.

"You broke it!" says Chet. "You broke my electric window!"

"Jerk!" says Tom. "You really are a problem child."

Things are not going well. Tom and Jerk should really not have broken the electric window on the Forces of Light's car. "I really don't believe this," Chet says. "You two just sit tight back there, would you?"

We drive along. I look over to see if Chet is mad.

But now Chet is smiling some secret smile.

Jerk is sitting back there, miserable.

The trees are black against the sky. We drive by what seems like mile after mile of etched branch and silent hill. We are not headed toward town. We've headed west.

Chet is humming one note. He doesn't ever stop to take in a breath. He hums his one note, and it rings in my ears.

Tom and Jerk have fallen sort of quiet.

Chet looks into the rear-view mirror. He says in a deep soft voice, "How are you two doing? Are you two feeling very sleepy?" No answer.

I look back. They are asleep.

Chet is looking at his watch. "We'll wake them up later. I shall erase their memories of me. Is the dog asleep?"

I twist my head and lean over the sticky leatherette. "It looks like it," I say.

"That gives us something to be thankful for," says Chet. "Now I'll explain what you need to do." He steers with one hand and reaches in his pocket with the other. He pulls out a blue velvet bag. "This I just traveled halfway across the universe for. It's the Arm of Moriator. Take it."

I take the bag from him. It's cold to the touch. When I pull open the drawstring, I see a glint of reflected light from inside.

"Look at it," Chet orders.

I empty the bag into my palm. The Arm of Moriator

does not look like an unusual object. It is a blue glass disk about three inches in diameter. There are four spidery characters spaced evenly around the edge of it. When we go over bumps, it rings lightly with the sound of someone rubbing a wet finger around the edge of the galaxy.

"What is it?" I ask, feeling confused and a little stupid.

"It is used as a lock to keep vast evil beings like Tch'muchgar chained in other worlds. Once it is activated, no evil being can touch it or shut it off. Let me explain." While Chet talks, I turn over the Arm of Moriator and hold it up so it catches oncoming headlights. When the light glints on it, it does nothing unusual. In the blue depths of it, I see nothing I wouldn't expect. Chet is saying, "When the vampires interrupt your town's spells of binding with their own spells, Tch'muchgar will try to leap from his world into yours. The Arm of Moriator will stop him. It will displace his world ever so slightly, which is like stopping an elevator between floors. He can step out, but there will be nothing there to step into. If he tries to leave his world, he'll walk into nothing. He will fall between realities. In other words, he will cease to exist."

I look at Chet carefully. "I thought that the Forces of Light didn't destroy anything. I thought that was against your rules."

"It is. This will merely act as a deterrent. Once he knows this is activated and in place, Tch'muchgar will never dare to leap out of his world. He knows that if he tries, he will annihilate himself."

We pull onto the highway.

I fumble with the shoulder strap to put the Arm in my pocket. "So how do I activate it?"

"Activation is easy and can be learned in a jiffy. Once you go into Tch'muchgar's world, all you have to do is touch each one of those four symbols around the edge in turn and say, 'Light, I invoke you.' Do you have that?"

"'Light, I invoke you'?"

"Yes. You've got it. You say that four times, touching one rune symbol each time. Then you can just drop the Arm. Is that clear?"

"But how do I know how to get into Tch'muchgar's world?"

"Ah!" says Chet, holding up a finger. "Ah! Here I have been particularly resourceful. I have approached the vampires, shown them that I am a being of great power, and convinced them that I am a demon in the service of one of Tch'muchgar's old friends, sent to help them."

"So you'll be with me?"

"Christopher, I'll be with you all the way," he reassures me warmly. "You don't have a thing to worry about. I'll introduce you to some of the vampires. They know me as Chet, too. We'll talk. Then we'll ask them to take us to the portal into Tch'muchgar's world. Then I'll stand by while you go into that world and activate the Arm. I'll be right there for you the whole time."

"But you aren't going in with me?"

"No. Tch'muchgar would recognize me immediately. I'll be waiting just outside. I'll use that sign on your arm to track you. After about two minutes, I'll pull you back out into this world."

We are spinning along the highway, passing the glowering taillights of trucks.

I urge nervously, "You'll be protecting me in there? I mean, all the time?"

Chet looks over at me, obviously concerned. "Hey, hey, of course, Christopher." He puts his hand on my wrist and gives it a firm squeeze. "I don't want you to worry about anything. You'll be perfect for this. I've told you. I'll protect you."

There is a certain feeling of adventure in the air. Chet tells me that I will not encounter much resistance, because he has thought it all out so cleverly. Being a vampire, I will just walk in through the assembly of vampires.

And now we are driving on the moonlit road toward the meeting place of vampires, and I am stunned that here I am and that a celestial being is at the wheel, glancing in the side mirrors to see what objects might be closer than they appear.

We are driving, and the great cliffs that were blasted out of quiet hills to make a way in the wilderness loom around us, striped with the smooth tracks of dynamite core. We drive, and I am sorry that my friends are asleep in the back and can't help, but at the same time, I am proud to be saving the world alone, with a sigil on my arm to ward off evil and a magic disk in my palm—and I look out the window and drink in the pines perched on a cliff edge, and the swoop of the hills, and the moon sailing over like the wise eye of the carp.

And we are turning off the highway and onto rambling back roads. And Chet sounds drunk with excitement, but quietly, as he says, "You should brace yourself for what you will see. The first time I went, the vampires had bodies under tarpaulins. I fear they enjoy grotesqueries in that general vein."

And he says to me, to buck me up, "Hey. I just made a pun."

And I say, "Yeah. That was a great pun you made there, Chet."

And he says, "Christopher, I'm beholden to you for mentioning it."

And we're driving on dark roads, past unknowing neighborhoods, and we're pulling up in front of a rundown church, where cars line the road beneath the pines—dark cars with license plates from many states—and now Chet is putting the black Cadillac into neutral, and park, and turning it off.

And I say to him, "Well, where to now?"

And he grins wolfishly and answers, "To hell and back."

We get out of the black Cadillac. The trees cluster thickly about us by the side of the road. The pavement is crumbling, and grass pokes through it.

Chet locks the doors, even though there is not much point (Jerk's window is wide open).

"Will the two of them be okay?" I ask.

Chet nods. "The vampires will assume I'm saving them for sometime when I come home late and just want something quick." He pockets his keys and rattles them.

The church looks like it was built sometime in the early sixties, and it has a wild sloping roof that peaks in a thin metal cross. The stained glass windows look like they're all just fragments of different colors, but I can't see too well because there's not much light coming from inside.

We walk up the flagstone path to the church. There must be a pond nearby, because I can hear the woody burping of the bullfrogs through the thick, dank forest.

The concrete of the church's basement level is chipped and dislocated. The wood is faded, and damp black cracks meander through it.

There are a few people lingering by the front door, at the top of some concrete steps. "Jill, I'm so happy to hear that," says the man.

"Isn't it great?" she says

Chet walks up the steps and says, "Bob! Jill!" and holds out his hand.

They say, "Hi, Chet!" and "Good to see you, Chet!" and shake his hand.

I am looking at them strangely because there is something wrong with the way they are. It's like a movement I can't detect, or a strange double shadow fizzing at the edge of their outline.

"This is Christopher," says Chet. "He's come to meet the whole gang."

They smile at me, and the Jill one says, "Great to have you—go right in," and we walk in.

Inside is a large parish hall with weighty curved beams arching across the roof. There's a buffet with lots of casseroles at one end, and ten tables have been set up and covered with paper tablecloths. The hall is filled with people. Some are sitting and laughing, eating green beans or talking and poking at the air with their plastic forks. Others are standing, holding styrofoam plates and laughing to one another. Some little toddlers are running from one end of the hall to the other, until a woman in a purple skirt and pink running shoes goes over and grabs one of their arms and I guess tells them to be quiet.

All of them have the double shadow, except some of the kids, and Chet. I squint to see if it goes away, but it doesn't.

Chet smiles and waves like a politician, and they look

at him sort of respectfully. I see a few teenagers over in one corner, whispering among themselves. The oldest one is an imposing guy of about eighteen or nineteen, who is wearing a jean jacket with the arms taken off. He has a bat tattoo on his upper arm. There are some girls standing around him, and I wonder if one of them is Lolli Chasuble.

"I'll be right back," says Chet to me. "Just sit down and try and be unobtrusive."

I am frightened, and I pull out a folding chair with a clattering that would be loud enough to wake the dead, if they weren't already serving themselves macaroni and cheese at the other end of the room. I sit down. I do not want the teenagers to come over and talk to me. I do not like meeting new people and always say something dumb. I especially hate meeting new people with fangs.

Chet has strolled across the room and is talking with some important-looking men.

Near me, there is a little girl in sagging brown leggings who is scraping her styrofoam plate with the edge of her fork. She pushes aside a chunk of cartilage and says to her father, "I'm done. Can I have more? Can I have more?"

He leans down close to the table and says precisely, "*May* I have more?"

I have figured out by now about the double shadows. Vampires. I must be able to see who is a vampire now that I am becoming one. This must be how that woman with the blonde hair saw me right before she was lynched. Vampiro-scopic vision. She must have thought I was a traitor because I was not helping her out. Maybe I *was* a traitor.

I look into the Dixie cups sitting on the table near me. They're filled with red punch. It looks like wild strawberry flavor.

I sniff it. It really is wild strawberry flavor. I don't understand why these vampires are eating human food. I make a mental note to ask Chet about it when we're alone.

"Ready?" says Chet, standing over me. Beside him is a man who looks like he is in his thirties, wearing a saggy European suit and a shirt with no collar. His hair goes down to his shoulders.

"Hi, Christopher," he says with a fake-o smile. "I'm Dr. Chasuble. You may have received a letter from my daughter?"

"Yes," I say. "It's nice to meet you. She has a way with colored pens."

He laughs, and I shake his hand, but suddenly I realize that I am sitting down and should be standing up to be polite. I stand up, but he's already stopped shaking my hand. Now the teenagers are staring at me. I can feel their interest and disdain.

"Shall we go in?" asks Chet.

"After you," says Dr. Chasuble, gesturing toward some double doors at the other end of the parish hall.

We walk down the length of the room, and I can tell people are staring at me. Some of them stop talking and lay their plastic forks down beside their plates. I am sweating, and I feel like I am very confused. The smell of the casseroles clogs my nostrils.

I say politely, "Mmm! Chicken casserole."

Chet's eyes are secretly dark, but he puts his arm around me and says brightly, "Christopher, that isn't chicken."

I look back at the room full of them eating it. I think of the father, bending low—"*May* I have some more?"—and I think of the cheesy flesh sliding down the child's gullet. I stop and stare; Chet pushes me on. We have arrived at the double doors. Dr. Chasuble opens them. We pass through a hall where the windows are broken, with webs of torn plastic strung over them to keep out the rain; a rotting corkboard is stuck full of messages held on with voodoo pins. We come to the far end of the hall, and Dr. Chasuble opens another door. Then we are in the sanctuary of the church of Tch'muchgar.

The church is tall and full of wine dark shadows.

The pews are empty. There are no hymnals or prayer books.

At the far end, up near the altar, three men are standing, their arms outstretched.

Among them floats an eye of red.

We walk up the aisle, our shoes clattering on the bare

floor. I can hear the thick breath going in and out of Dr. Chasuble's nostrils.

I'm electric with vertigo, even though I'm on the ground, vertigo like I felt once when I stood on the edge of a high cliff in Arizona and looked straight down. I keep swallowing, but my throat is dry.

We approach the eye, a burned hole in the air. There are crates opened, filled with paper sacks of powders and chalks. Books lie open on the floor. Standing around the dais limply, like ungainly storks in a mire, are twelve abandoned music stands. On several of them there are yellow Schirmer & Co. music scores, which say in blue writing *Maruczek: Eight Atonal Chants for Unhallowed Liturgies, Winds and Mixed Chorus.*

The eye glows red among the three men. Their sleeves are drawn back, and they have scratched bleeding symbols in their forearms.

There is a hum, as of energy.

"I'll take over from here," says Chet. "The Melancholy One wishes to meet this child."

I am feeling sick. I cannot tell what is happening to me.

"All right. Please," says Dr. Chasuble to the three men.

Chet has moved to the center, by the eye, and he is spinning it between his hands like one of those tops on a string, spinning it so it burns more redly, and lights his polka-dot tie, and grows, and spits sparks.

The three men lower their hands and move away.

"Come on," says Dr. Chasuble, gesturing to the men.

"Five minutes," says Chet. "He should be indoctrinated by then."

And suddenly, I am afraid of him.

The others are shuffling back along the aisle. Chet still stands, his eyes closed, massaging the eye, and I suspect it is the gateway to Tch'muchgar's world.

The pool of light is growing larger and larger, and now I can hear it moaning with energy, and I am wondering whether to make a break for it.

I do not know what to do. Suddenly I am unsure of it all, and I realize that if Chet is not what he seems, I am lost. If he is not from the Forces of Light, then I am tiny in the jaws of an evil god, and I don't know what to do with the disk that I have now clutched in my hand, a disk that might not do what Chet says at all. I look at his grimacing, twitching mouth and his spinning fingers.

"Go on," says Chet. He opens his eyes and looks at me. "Go on. Quickly. Where angels fear to tread."

I stand there. The roof of the church is dark and about me like vast moldy wings. I can hear, as if I were underwater, the distorted sounds of singing and talking from the other room.

"Enter," hisses Chet. "Enter, now."

"Should I—?"

"Enter. Walk. Drop the Arm."

I am frightened.

"Get going," he says, almost baring his teeth. "This isn't easy. Come on, you—good god, your world is . . . Would you go?"

I balk—"Get in there," Chet demands. "Now. Or we'll never believe you want your vampirism cured, and the whole deal's off."

"Chet—," I say, backing away.

"Your only hope. Our only hope."

"Please can I—"

"Go!"

There's nothing else to do.

So I step into the circle.

And I drop through space without time, and I am in Tch'muchgar's world.

# CHAPTER 5 Darkness and wet.

For a minute, I just hang there and wonder where I am.

Like being under the reservoir in winter, I realize. Hanging far beneath the ice, while above it is a bleak day and the leaves are on the ground and the waters are dead and the trees are just streaks of brown scraped on the plain white sky.

Down here, there is nothing to see; no motion anywhere. No light at all.

But this, if it were a lake, and not a world, would be a lake with no bottom, and no surface, and there is no life within it. I can feel that. I can still feel the vertigo in my toes, as they hang in nothing, and I know that this murky world spreads out dark and dead into infinity.

Though I am hanging in what feels like water, it must not be water. It feels thicker for one thing, as if I were dunked in embalming fluid. For another thing, I do not choke when I breathe it.

This infinite lake is empty, has never known life, except that somewhere Tch'muchgar must be lying, waiting for his release. I can hear a distant noise, or perhaps it is in my head, the static from his thoughts, like the far-off hum of a highway when you're snorkeling deep in the coldest part of the lake. A sound or sense like the thrumming, again and again, of military trucks in a convoy rumbling over a distant bridge.

If I can hear him, I wonder if he can hear me.

I have the Arm in my hand. I feel around the edge for the first rune. I touch it and whisper, "Light, I invoke you."

The second rune. "Light, I invoke you."

The third. "Light, I invoke you."

The fourth. "Light, I invoke you."

And with that, the disk starts to glow, and a voice faintly says all around me, "Activated."

As Chet has told me to do, I release the disk. Then I reach out and impulsively clutch it (the blue light picking my fingers out of the murk)—I may have made a mistake.

Have I? I don't know. What else, I wonder, can I do? Tentatively, I push it out into the void.

It floats away, but I can't tell how fast, or how far away it is from me. The light continues in the darkness, lighting nothing, drifting.

I hang there for a minute. Chet will pull me out. This is what he has told me.

And I start to realize that, though there could be no breeze here, and though there is no life to stir the water, the plasma all around me is starting to move and eddy.

The sound is approaching me, too. Getting louder. I am in the midst of something. Everything is thickening.

It is then that I realize that the movements themselves are the thoughts of great Tch'muchgar, all around me, vast, rebounding. I am in the midst of him. The Vampire Lord is thinking; and I can feel the currents of his thoughts slither and snake around me like a cluster of prying water moccasins.

I start flailing my arms and shouting. My arms can hardly trawl through the thick slime; my legs kick against nothing; and still the curious currents crawl and prod me and slink up and down my face and legs, the thoughts and sardonic bemusements of the Vampire Lord.

He is all around me, and I can hardly move for the density of him. His thoughts break against my head like waves. He does not care much that I am there; I am so tiny, and his thoughts spread out all around me for miles and depths beyond reckoning.

I stop struggling. I hang there. I try not to move; not to breathe. Everything I breathe would be Tch'muchgar; everything I touch. And still the thoughts wash around me, the bored, bitter, mordant thoughts of the trapped Vampire Lord.

*Out.*

*How long. Much longer? How long. How.*

*God I hate it. God I hate.*

*There is defeat so deep.*

*I hate. Damn you. All.*

Once I stood with Paul in early spring and heard the reservoir's ice crack, heard the reverberations tick and moan through the black wet branches of the trees. Those were like Tch'muchgar's thoughts — vast voiced sounds that echoed on the hills, scolded the woods, called to the empty pines.

*A lifetime spent with nothing*—he thinks.

*Circle and circle and circle. God when how long. How long? God when.*

*Hate it. Hate it. Hate.*

*Circle and circle.*

*Oh, hello.*

I stiffen.

*Oh, hello, boy. Oh, hello.*

*Who are you? Who are you? I am trapped. Will you release me?*

*Will you?*

*I am trapped. Will you?*

*Do you know what it is like?*

I am desperate for Chet. I start to kick again. I start to kick and struggle in the darkness.

*You cannot struggle. That is what it is like. Cannot move. Here. Here.*

And the substance all around me thickens, and it is like I am locked in a glacier, a tiny thing locked in a glacier, and so far away from anyone. And somewhere life is going on with trees, but I am frozen, lost, miles deep and so far north it is a north that is never seen, howling storms, silence, and I will be there always—

Like being buried alive—buried alive in a coffin so narrow I can't even fold my arms; I can't lift my hands without banging my wrists. I can't shift my hips. I can't move my head from side to side. I can't move my toes, though they're stubbed against the lid, some up, some down. And I can smell all around me, dark and immovable, thick dirt, crowding—but know I'll never rise or sleep or die. Staring straight. Can't budge. Itching. Feel the earth spread out, foot by foot, so many feet up to the surface, so many, foot after foot after foot, the grass—never hear—never—

*Stay boy—*

*Ha! Stay!*

—never hear—

*Down!*

—trapped—

*Stay!*

And then Chet sends for me.

I feel the sigil on my arm pulsing with light.

I feel the red glow of the portal all around me.

It seeps into my bones, the sweet air of earth, and warms my muscles, draws me out—

—away from the dark—

—across time and space I fly, shooting, wafting, away from the laughter of Tch'muchgar, the confinement, through ages I tumble—

—and fall down on my knees

—before the well-shined brogues of Chet the Celestial Being.

● ◑ ☾

"Ahhh . . . ," he says, and smiles. He stops gesturing with his hands. He lets them drop to his sides, and the portal stops snapping and popping and dwindles. "How was the other world?" asks Chet.

"Oh, god," I gasp unresponsively. "Oh, god."

"You can't make an omelet without breaking eggs," says Chet.

"Thank you for the cooking tip," I say. "It was a nightmare."

I'm huddled on the floor. My clothes aren't even wet, which is strange, and I am no longer feeling trapped in a glacier; and Chet pulled me out, so it looks like he really is a celestial being, and I'm so happy I could just sit down and write a show tune about it all. "How much time's passed?" I ask.

Chet looks at his watch and says, "About two minutes. Jet lag?"

"God," I say, shaking myself. I can't get up. "It was awful. Really awful."

"When you're ready, they're waiting for us outside."

"Who?"

Chet puts his hands in his pockets, so his jacket bunches above his wrists. "Dr. Chasuble and his vampiric sorcerers," he explains. "They're here preparing the spells of interruption to disrupt the spells of imprisonment your mayor and local clergy will be casting at the Sad Festival of Vampires. But now, thanks to you, Tch'muchgar can't make a move. Even if the vampires do succeed in opening a dimensional gate large enough to get him through, he still has to stay put. If he tries to jump from that world to this, the Arm will displace his world and terminate him completely. He'll exit that world and won't enter another."

He lends me a hand to stand. I say, "So I've just saved the world?"

Chet chuckles and knocks me on the shoulder. "Listen to you!" he says. "Yes, you could put it that way."

"Okay. Don't knock me on the shoulder, please. I feel really, really sick."

Chet glances up toward the double doors leading out of the sanctuary. "Then let's get out of here. Vampires have no sympathy for the expulsion of food. They're very ingestion oriented."

As I stand there in that dank and grave-chilled sanctuary, I feel almost drunk with a sudden realization: In an hour, I figure, we'll be well away from here and Chet will have cured me of my curse forever. Good-bye, vampires. Good-bye, midnight hour. Good-bye, Tch'muchgar, the Melancholy One, Vampire Lord.

We walk back down the aisle. Over in the side aisle, rolled up, lies a mildewed cloth banner with faceless felt figures in bright colors. A stack of songbooks leans up against a wall. Someone has poured a bucket of red paint all over them.

In the hallway, one of the men with the bleeding arms leans up against the window frame, smoking.

"Christopher has spoken with the Melancholy One," Chet announces beatifically.

Several men walk over. They all look at me. I nod.

"Shit, great," says the guy smoking the cigarette. "What . . . I mean, what did he say?"

Chet looks at me, scratching the corner of his mouth with his pinkie.

I squirm for a minute. Then I say, "He proclaims that he shall lead us all to Victory. With a capital V."

Dr. Chasuble looks at the others. "Great!" he says.

"Yeah, great!"

Dr. Chasuble, Chet, and I go back into the parish hall. Everyone looks up at us. Dr. Chasuble and Chet smile at them to reassure them. Some of them smile back, and on so many faces, I see fangs.

What looks like a middle-aged lady dressed in cornflower blue rayon slacks is standing by the food table as we pass. "Go well?" she asks.

"Yes, indeed," says Chet.

She gestures toward the two casseroles. "Would you like some of Jennifer or Dave?"

"No, thanks," says Chet.

She looks at me and offers, "Jennifer Carreiras, fifteen, of Haverhill, or Dave Philips, fifty-three, of Springfield? Dave has a broccoli garnish, and Jenn has Doris Blum's special cornflakes crust—lots of crunchy bits."

"No, thanks," says Chet. "We have someone waiting for us out in the car."

"Oh! Bon appètit," says the woman in cornflower blue.

The teenagers are staring at me from their corner. The kid with the tattoo has tilted back in his chair and is looking at me enviously and with a little bit of hate. I want to get the hell out of there.

Dr. Chasuble is talking quietly with Chet as we walk out. They talk about the technical aspects of spells and when spells are to be cast.

We are outside. A chill wind is blown in rags and tatters through the trees. One lone frog is belching in the swamp.

Suddenly, I say to Dr. Chasuble, "I thought you only sucked blood. Why are you eating flesh?"

He looks at me curiously for a second. "We," he says softly. "Not 'you.'"

I can tell Chet is angry about the slip.

The bullfrog calls through the trees.

Dr. Chasuble says, "Eating flesh is a disgusting habit. I agree. We do it mostly for the little ones, the kids, when they haven't yet become vampiric. It's important to accustom them to the idea of taking human life for food. Otherwise, they can prove very dangerous and difficult to the family when puberty hits."

Chet nods. "The family that preys together, stays together."

Dr. Chasuble laughs and puts his arm around my shoulder. "But look. Forget about eating. Drinking—

that's the thing. Exsanguination—draining blood—is a beautiful act, Christopher. At first, of course, it will be messy. Before you get the hang of it, you'll gag, and lap, but after a while you'll learn how to really use your fangs to your best advantage. When you're a real pro, the pumping of the heart will send the blood squirting right into your mouth. Effortless. Sweet. Thick. Tart.

"And then it's a beautiful moment. Lying on top of someone, feeling the quivering of their heart and just slowly, smoothly, silently pulling their lifeblood out of them. It's a very gentle-feeling death. Eventually, they just stop struggling."

He stands back from me. The frog is silent in his pond. "And remember," he says. "Lolli is up for a date whenever you want to have your first experience. I imagine Chet can teach you a thing or two, but Lolli has a good head on her shoulders and can show you the ropes. If you don't feed soon, your blood-lust is going to become overpowering, your fangs will come out, and people will start to notice things."

Chet holds out his hand. "We'll be in touch," he says.

"Chet," says Dr. Chasuble, shaking.

"Nice to meet you," I say.

"And we'll be in touch, too," says Dr. Chasuble. "Hope you'll join us during the Sad Festival of Vampires. Long reign Tch'muchgar."

"Long reign Tch'muchgar," I agree hastily.

"Hey, ditto," says Chet the Celestial Being.

We walk down the drive toward Chet's car.

Tom and Jerk are toppled in the back seat. Jerk has curled up awkwardly with his cheek on his knee, and there is drool on the denim.

Without talking, Chet starts the car, puts it into drive, and heads back down the cracked road. We drive for a ways before we start to pass small bungalows in the woods, some of them with sagging aluminum toolsheds or car trailers for boats, resting on the pine needles.

Chet seems mildly triumphant. "Very well done," he says. "You cut it a bit fine there at the end. With the 'you.'"

"Now do you cure my vampirism?" I ask.

"Yes, of course," says Chet. "I'll send someone around. I'm not authorized to do it myself. But I'll arrange for an annulment of the curse. Do you know your social security number?"

"No," I say.

"Hm," he says, pondering as he taps on the steering wheel. "It may take a couple extra days then. But there will be someone, don't worry."

"Have you figured out any more about how I got cursed?" I ask. "I mean, I don't think I've ever been bitten or anything."

"No, I haven't. As to guesses? Difficult to say. It might have been years ago, and it's just taking effect now because of puberty and hormonal changes, sort of like asthma or allergies. In any event, we'll have you fixed up in a jiffy."

We approach the highway. And we are soaring along it, the wind whiffling in through the back window.

We drive along, and I am half dazed by what I have seen. In my head I am picturing what I will be able to say to Rebecca during the Sad Festival of Vampires: We are standing by the reservoir, and the air of the summer's night is as sweet as wine, and she's saying, "Come on. Did you really enter Tch'muchgar's world and set in place the seed of his destruction?"

"Yes!" I say, laughing. "Didn't I just say that?"

"You did just say that, but also you were lying."

"I was not lying."

"Okay. You weren't lying."

And her soft face is lit by the fireworks going off above, as the towering vampire Tch'muchgar explodes above the lake. There are vampire parts blowing up every which way, and he's yodeling as he blows up and falls in sizzling chunks into the reservoir. People on the beaches lie together with their head in one another's lap, or lean against one another, and when Tch'muchgar does a particularly colorful explosion, everyone says, "Oooh! Aaah!"

And I turn to Rebecca and look at her smoky eyes and her careful lips, and I feel the warmth of her against me. We lie stretched out beneath the trees, looking up at the stars and the exploding Vampire Lord, and our thoughts are so content and similar that they rub up against each other like cats.

I sit up. The car is idling, sitting on the dark lane near the water tower. Chet has undone his seat belt and is twisted in his seat. His arms shoot backward, and his fingers are pressed against Tom's and Jerk's foreheads.

"We'll set them where they were. Erase their memories. Then you can rejoin them."

I look into the tangled woods. "What about that Thing that was stalking me? With the alien toupee?"

"Don't worry," says Chet. "It can't touch you. And anyway, it's not in the woods anymore."

"Thank goodness," I say.

"It's at your house." He lifts his fingers off their foreheads. Jerk's skin is so pasty the fingers have left red welts. "Okay, boys. Get out of the car and walk into the woods that way. Then why don't you come to your senses. You're looking for Christopher."

In a matter-of-fact kind of way, as if they were getting out to run into McDonald's, Tom and Jerk open the doors and get out. They don't speak, but they shake their limbs uncomfortably.

"And take the damn dog."

Jerk reaches in and pulls at Bongo's collar. Bongo is whining. It sounds like someone scrubbing a window.

Together, they walk off into the woods.

"What am I going to do?" I ask. "That Thing's waiting for me!"

Chet shakes his head. "It can't touch you, because I have my mark on you. The Thing is just observing you. Trying to figure out what we're up to. Are you going to get out, too? I think you'll want to walk home with the others for company."

So I get out, too. I shut my door behind me.

"Good night," says Chet, leaning down to call through the window. "And good job. With saving the world, I mean. We'll send someone around soon about the vampirism, and I'll come by if I have the time."

Suddenly, I have a very suspicious feeling. Chet is waving and smiling. His smile is very fake.

"Wait!" I say.

But he is still waving, and the window is rolling up, and he pulls out onto the road and drives off.

"Wait! Chet! I can't sleep! Please! I can hardly eat!"

I listen to the motor fade down the lane as the car rolls past broken stone walls.

"Chet!"

The lights of his car disappear.

"Damn."

I walk into the woods.

I cannot place where I am.

Then I hear Tom and Jerk thrashing in the distance.

I run toward them.

They are standing in the woods, looking for the road with the flashlight.

"Where were you?" says Tom, as I run up. He looks confused and a little frightened, as if he can't remember something, but won't admit it.

"Over there," I answer; but I don't point anywhere.

It takes us about half an hour to find our way home Bongo has quieted down by now. He is exhausted. We go under the railroad bridge. We drop Jerk off at his house and tell him we'll see him tomorrow. We hear him crooning to the dog as he goes inside that it's feeding time for Bongo; that Bongo is a good boy.

We walk back to Tom's. I call my father for a ride.

Who knows what is happening. Who knows whether Chet is on the level, and who knows whether I have just made an error and given Tch'muchgar some hideous tool for evil, and who knows when I shall be cured and be able to sleep again soundly.

My father comes to get me.

Now the classic rock station is playing hits from the seventies.

My father doesn't know the words, so he cannot sing along.

# CHAPTER 6

Once the rains have stopped, the things that were dead start growing.

The blossoms come out in the orchards. They are wrapped around the trees like great white smothering sheets. And there are streets where tree after tree is the bright unnatural pink of circus candy. You can almost hear madcap carousel music just looking at the pink trees drifting by the bus.

The earth is giving birth to insects. At first, there are only a few mosquitoes. Then the swamp starts disgorging them as if spitting watermelon seeds. Little heat-seeking watermelon seeds, spat from between its gap-toothed grin. Flies bounce against the windows. Moths hit the screens at night. Ants are in our Life cereal, marching five by five and six by six, like in the song.

Dead fish lap at the edges of the reservoir. I don't understand their life cycle, but maybe they waited all winter to die, or maybe their flat corpses have been stacked under the ice all winter like TV dinners and just now floated to the top.

I can't believe Chet has abandoned me again. I am sure he will be back like he promised, but it would just make me feel better if I knew. I wish I could get in touch with him. Strange things are happening to my body.

Things are twisting and poking in my mouth, and I have an orthodontist's appointment coming up.

The Thing with the One-Piece Hair appears and disappears without warning. Some days it is there, staring, following me to school, leaving no crushed footprints as it trudges across the grass. Sometimes I do not see it for days on end.

At night sometimes, when I can't sleep, I get up and go to the window. The Thing stands there, below, beneath the lamppost, on the spot where Jon Edwards broke his arm two years ago on a skateboard while saying the words, "I go as fast as spitfire!"

When I am feeling all alone at two or three in the morning, sometimes I wave to the unmoving, unholy Thing. Hello, Mr. Thing with the One-Piece Hair!

As Chet promised, it does nothing to harm me now. It does nothing but watch and wait.

But still, I am wondering when it is going to make its move.

I am almost more worried when I don't see it there.

Then it could be anywhere.

Jerk is worried about me. I can see it in his eyes. He's no longer just hurt when I ignore him and walk an alternate route so that I won't have to speak to him. He thinks I wouldn't do that normally.

I hope I wouldn't, but I feel so sleepy during the day—because I can't sleep at night—that I don't want to waste my energy. Of course, talking to Jerk is not a waste of energy, especially if you would like to hear an imitation of late night comedy show reruns, but I don't see what there's to gain from it.

I do feel bad that Tom has abandoned him, too. Tom doesn't have an excuse. I guess the three of us are just growing apart. Tom is hanging out more and more with the cooler crowd.

It isn't difficult to be a cooler crowd than Jerk. All you have to do is not sniff your own underarms at lunchtime.

Without me, Tom just doesn't want to be around Jerk anymore.

Sometimes Jerk will see that Tom is talking to the other kids in that group he's with, and Jerk will drift beside them. He'll stand right there on the edge, behind everyone else, resting his hand nervously on one of the chair backs, and his eyes will flip from speaker to speaker, hoping one will say something he can add to. When they all start making jokes, he'll make a quick one, too; he repeats his jokes four or five times, just to make sure everyone's heard it. He punctuates them with "yeah!"; for example, "And then he falls and breaks his leg, yeah! Like, then he falls and breaks his leg, yeah! And then, like, he falls and breaks his leg."

They are polite people, so they don't tell him to go away

I want to be one of them. They are good looking. They know secrets about one another's dating lives. They laugh together in public spaces.

Plus, Rebecca Schwartz is one of them. I wish Tom would draw me over to talk with her. He knows I have this crush on her.

But Tom doesn't want to be seen with me either. I still am sure he knows something, but the question is how much. He keeps saying that I haven't been normal lately, that I've been completely weird. He says I need some sleep and that I'm always, like, a complete downer nowadays.

He is right. Tom is right on these points.


I am staring at my clock.

It flashes. It says 3:52.

3:52.

3:52.

That is no time to be awake. It is the rawest hour of the earthly day. There is no one to help you at 3:52. Many people don't even exist at 3:52.

A crow caws somewhere.

My braces hurt. The ache is dull and continuous.

I push back my covers. I'm getting too hot.

I can't sleep, and I'm so thirsty. I'm tired of those words, "I'm so thirsty." They are dull, dull, dull. I don't know what to do. That's what I keep thinking. I don't know whether to trust Chet. He could be a double agent. I don't know what he's doing if he is a double agent. I lie there wondering what he could be doing. Why would he ask me to place the Arm of Moriator, a device for the Forces of Light, in Tch'muchgar's world if he is a servant of Darkness? Unless the Arm of Moriator is not what he said it was, and it is some dire magical engine with a dark purpose. Could be! I do not want to think about that. I writhe around in bed. I try not to think about it. Not to think about it at all.

The space between my teeth and my cheeks is dry. I pull up saliva from under my tongue. It shoots back down the channels on either side of my jaw.

My braces ache dully.

The flaps on the inside of my cheeks are still dry. I suck up more saliva to wet them. It's as sluggish as a putty shake.

I am getting angry now. I sit up. The walls are too close around me. Somewhere there is a cool, wet, open expanse and I want to be there. I am irate at my saliva.

I stand up. I walk over to my window and slide it open. I breathe in the night air.

Hopeless. Thin as nothing.

I want to pound on something and make it bleed for me. I want to tear into something. I want to tear away these walls.

I need to go to the bathroom. There's water there.

The pain from my braces shoots through the bone of my jaw. My teeth are moving.

I reach out for my door handle.

Then I hold up my arm, close to my eyes.

My pajama sleeve has been pressed into a slinkie of ringlets at the elbow. My forearm is bare before it.

At the sight of my smooth white skin, fine as cream, I start to salivate. I trace the little blue veins from the wrist up to the plumper muscle.

I lower my mouth. My open lips just nuzzle my forearm.

The points of my canines touch the bare skin. My canines seem larger than usual. My saliva is thick.

Helplessly, I pierce the skin; and helplessly, I start drawing and sucking as ferociously as I can, yanking blood up into my mouth. The pain jolts my elbow up and down, while I feel the blessed blood murmuring over my lips, my chin, down—in the most tantalizing trickle—my throat, a few drops, a spot, more; and I tear at my arm and slash downward with the teeth, rutting up little tracks of meat while the thick, sour tang of my own gore sweetly fills my mouth and cheeks, puffing them out. It hurts like the devil, and I'm moaning, lost in pain and wonder, but now I hack a little more at my arm with the same pleasure I'd peel a scab, so the pain is bigger, harder, cleaner, more burning, more scathing, more cleansing.

Lost in pleasure and pain, I almost howl, slurping, licking, and my arm is red and slick and I chase every, every, every last drop.

A half hour later, I am lying drowsily on the floor.

My braces are just one big loopy tangle. My pajamas are twisted all around me. There are wide swaths of blood scraped across my striped arms and chest. The wounds in my left arm have clotted and started to heal. Very quickly, I notice. Unnaturally quickly. My fangs have slid back into my gums.

I curl up like a kitten.

For the first time in weeks I sleep, satiated.

My teeth ground me for a week. My teeth are fine, but my braces were yanked completely off my canines. I told people it was a night-time skateboarding accident. My orthodontist says this is unlikely. He has taken the braces off entirely. My mother says she is grounding me for a week or until I tell her what really happened. She thinks I got in a fight with a gang.

"Yes, Mom," I say. "Luckily, I fended them off single-handedly."

She says, "You have got an attitude problem."

My orthodontist took her aside and spoke to her. That I know. I do not know what he said. She says it was serious.

They are starting to suspect me, I can tell. Not of the right things—my father keeps leaning close to me to casually smell my breath—but they suspect me none the less.

I want Chet to come back.

I have a feeling he is not coming.


The lawns are starting to smell syrupy sweet. In the next week or so, many of the blossoms on the trees change to leaves, however that works.

The leaves are so fragile, an infant green, they look almost frightened when they first cluster at the joints and elbows of the trees in the yard.


All I seem to see on the news are stories about people killing inhumans. I've never noticed it so much before. There are still all the same stories about starvation, and fighting in the Middle East, and senators talking about the national debt—but now I notice more than I ever did before those other stories about the mobs, the lynchings, all over America.

I see the deaths of vampires, as much as can be shown; and I watch the televised burning of witches. I see the chasing of warlocks through main streets in Iowa. And then there are the Abominations of Slanterville, a town in Florida that is found to be filled with worshippers of an alligator-god named Slundge. Federal agents were lowered in on bungee cords from helicopters and they captured the townspeople, who had bred with beasts of the swamp to produce squalling children with mongrel patches of scale and horn. The people of Slanterville, down to the rat-tailed babies, were sent to prison, and their town was burned in the night.

"I don't know why the Feds didn't just kill those Abominations," says my mother idly as she passes in front of the TV, feeding herself Cheetos. "It's not like they could ever lead normal lives."

In prison, away from the swamps, the Abominations started to weaken and get sick. A fight broke out. I guess some human inmates claimed that the Abominations of Slanterville hogged the showers. The fight turned into a riot, and within fifteen minutes all the Abominations in the male ward had been beaten to death. The riot spread. More people were killed. In a prison riot, the first to die are the inhumans. The Abominations, the trolls, the changelings, the demon-possessed.

I can't believe I'm one of a hated race, too. It doesn't matter that I'm a half-vampire and they're Abominations. We are all hated. We are brethren in being hated. I watch the human inmates brandishing bloody instruments, waving them in triumph, and I can't understand why they hate me so much. I have done nothing. It is like they are saying, "We're coming for you next, boy. We know your zip code; we're on our way. We'll kill you all."

But then I think, *I am not inhuman yet.*

I will not be a killer; I will not give them reason to hate me.

I feel people's eyes on me all the time. "Why are you watching that gruesome footage?" my mother asks. "You want your brain to turn to mush?"

And when I keep watching I notice her lingering by the door, looking at me as if she's worried about me. She's worried about why I have to keep staring at these scenes. I can't pay attention to the screen when she looks at me that way because I'm too busy being looked at. I just sit there, not looking back, hoping she'll go away, and I wonder: What is the difference between the look of a parent who is concerned and the look of a parent who is suspicious?

She doesn't look concerned or suspicious when my brother watches riot footage, because he talks constantly about the media and the splicing techniques.

She almost glares at me, though, as if she knows, maybe somewhere deep within her, that what I'm watching is myself being killed on screen. I'm staring at it because I need to know what might happen to me. I need to understand why I am hated.

I keep telling myself that it will not happen, that soon this will all be a memory.

But I do not know when Chet is coming; or why he would come; or if he is coming at all.

Peeper frogs are starting to chirp in the woods. The sunlight is bright through the leaves of the oaks. My brother is out there, in the back yard, filming slugs.

He has a big biology project to do. He decided to do a science documentary on the life cycle of the slug. That way he can work with video equipment and lots of gastropods.

I am lying upstairs on my bed, trying to get some sleep. Through my open window, I can hear my brother's voice. "Establishing shot. The lawn," he says. "A fearsome jungle for the average garden slug."

Somewhere downstairs, my mother is talking on the phone, comparing her antidepressant brand with her friends'.

It has been some time since I've slept. I hate the sunlight, now. It makes me weary.

I am trying to fall asleep, but I can still feel the dull thirst sucking at my upper palate. Everything bothers me. The glint of light from my posters. The hiccupping, nervous chirp of the peepers. The distant rumble of a lawn mower.

Something shifts over near my desk.

I turn the other way and jam my wrist in my ear. I close my eyes. My arm is uncomfortable, twisted so my wrist will fit in my ear. I turn the other way.

Something scuffs the rug.

I open my eyes. A man is in my room, staring down at me.

I sit up, yelping. It is the Thing with the One-Piece Hair. It approaches me. Its hands are spread outward, ten fingers raised in a fan. It has no expression on its face.

"No! Shit! Get out!" I scream, scrabbling with my sleeve to reveal Chet's symbol.

The Thing keeps walking toward me.

"What's your problem?" calls Paul. "Can you shut up?"

"Christopher," says the Thing with the One-Piece Hair in its voice like many speaking. "Do not be alarmed or attempt to flee. I am a servant of the Forces of Light."

I babble, "No, you're not! You broke in! Get out! You're . . . This is illegal!"

"I am a servant of the Forces of Light, and I have been instructed to approach you."

"No, you're not!" I scream, holding out the sigil on my arm. "Get out! You can't do this! This—this is breaking and entering."

It gazes at me. "As I am a five-dimensional construct, the concept of 'entering' has no useful application in this scenario." It walks toward my bed. Its knees are by the edge of the bed. It bends down over me so its dead eyes are close to my face. I can smell its steely breath as it speaks.

"Get out!" I scream. "Help! Help!"

The door slams open against the wall. My mother storms into the room. "Chris!" she says. "Good god, what's wrong?"

"Help me! It!" I say, inarticulately.

"What?"

"Hey, what's the matter?" yells Paul from the lawn. "You okay in there?"

"He's fine," my mother calls. "A nightmare or something."

"As you may observe, calling for help was ill advised and futile," the Thing points out, straightening up.

"Chris, what's the matter?" my mother asks, concerned.

The Thing is prattling obliviously, "I have come to make inquiries of the whereabouts of the Arm of Moriator, which was taken illegally from our arsenal twenty-eight days ago."

"The Arm . . . it was taken illegally?" I stutter. "I-I mean . . ."

"Who are you talking to?" my mother asks. "Hello? Earth to Chris."

"Never mind," I say to her. "I'm fine now."

"You're fine now. Great. Why is this family so crazy? Why, and I ask why, is this family so crazy?"

"You have seen the Arm of Moriator?" asks the Thing.

I nod.

"Who are you nodding at?" asks my mother. "Who are you nodding at?" She shakes her head. "I don't know. Chris, why don't you come out and talk to us like a normal human being when you're done being a psychopath. Okay?" She closes the door behind her.

The Thing starts in again. "You have been in contact with a being of some power. I encountered him and attempted to warn you that harm would come if you assisted him. Please identify this being."

The Thing waits.

"His name is Chet," I say.

"His name is not Chet. Chet is not his name at all."

"If you know . . ."

"His name is a pattern of thought. You cannot replicate it?"

"No," I say. "I guess we weren't formally introduced. I mean, by brain or anything."

"He remains unidentified. His purpose is unclear. You will now clarify?"

My jaw opens and closes while I think. I am frightened, but my mind is working quickly. What can I safely tell the Thing with the One-Piece Hair, I wonder—and does it serve Light or Darkness?

"There are some vampires," I say. "He promised me . . . Well, anyway, these vampires, they're trying to cast a spell that will interfere with the rituals for binding Tch'muchgar."

"Continue."

I hesitate. I can't explain about where the Arm is. If the Thing is evil, it might not know yet about the Arm. I don't know who I can trust. Chet is not here. For all I know, Chet is not anywhere.

"How do I know you're from the Forces of Light?" I ask.

"We do not require that you believe us."

"Who are you? Why have you been following me?"

"I repeat: I am a servant of the Forces of Light. Twenty-eight days ago the being you refer to verbally as 'Chet' entered our arsenal and, deceiving us as to his identity, received the Arm of Moriator for what he termed a highly secret mission. He explained that you were to be the human operative for the Forces of Light. For some days, we did not suspect anything. Then it came to our attention that there was no such mission authorized by our higher authorities. We believed there was some error. I was sent to monitor your activities and report back. Having followed you for some time, I reported that it did not seem you were engaged in any destructive activity. As it is inobvious how the Arm of Moriator could be used for evil, we concluded that you were in fact working for the powers of Light and that we had made some error."

The Thing turns its left profile toward me and continues. "Seventeen days ago 'Chet' attempted to get in contact with you to give you the Arm. This time, I immediately sensed that he was a powerful negative being, and I approached you to question you about him. Before I could speak with you, he arrived and incapacitated me."

The Thing shifts its head again to present its right profile. "Since then, I have continued to monitor your activities to establish to what extent you were in collusion with 'Chet.' In spite of your vampirism, I have reached the conclusion that you were most likely deceived as well and are not knowingly in the service of Darkness. For this reason, I approach you now in an attempt to establish the whereabouts of the Arm of Moriator and 'Chet's' possible motives in stealing it."

The Thing stands there and waits.

Finally, I admit, "Yes, he tricked me. He told me he was from the Forces of Light."

"He is not from the Forces of Light."

"I know. He just said that to—"

"We have evidence that he is working for the Forces of Darkness. Explain."

"I was saying. He wanted me to activate the Arm of Moriator for him."

"The Arm is dangerous to powerful spiritual beings of Darkness and its activation can result in their annihilation. Explain his application."

"He wanted me to . . ." I hesitate. Then, in a shaky voice, I ask, "If I tell you all this, are you going to cure my vampirism?"

"That is of secondary importance."

"Please," I say. "I need to know that you're going to help me."

"I repeat that that is of secondary importance. Please continue."

"Not until you've told me you can help me."

"You are in no position to bargain. You may have compromised the security of your nation and our cause. In the event of noncompliance, you could be reported to the local human authorities. You will continue your explanation."

"If you're from the Forces of Light, you're supposed to want to help me!" I protest angrily.

"We care deeply about the future of the human race. You are not currently of the human race. Your actions, in keeping with your vampirism, may well have compromised the security of your nation and our cause."

I'm crouched there on my bed, fuming, sulking.

"You will continue your explanation."

"Okay, I'll tell you, but you better help!"

"We will do our utmost in the event that this situation can be resolved to our satisfaction. Our aim is to ensure that the imprisonment and torture of Tch'muchgar the Vampire Lord continue indefinitely. Any aid you provide in furthering that aim will be seen as evidence of good faith. You will continue your explanation."

"Chet asked me—"

"One moment and I will record this statement."

"What?"

There is a click from within the Thing. "Continue," it says. "Recording."

"I was saying, the being I call 'Chet'—"

There is a whisper of air. My mattress bobs slightly.

I swivel.

Chet himself is there, standing grimly on my bed, his arms crossed.

He stares down at the two of us. His shoes bite deeply into my blankets. He looks darkly at me, then turns to the Thing. "Deceiving the poor boy," he chastens. "Is there nothing you wicked, wicked people won't stoop to?"

I'm trapped between them. I don't know which way to go.

Chet says, "Christopher, get away from it. It means you harm."

"Identify yourself," the Thing demands, backing up warily. "Identify."

"Christopher, stand up and go over by that wall."

I scramble to the edge of the bed and fall off the end. "Wait," I say to Chet. "It's accusing you—"

"I know what it's saying. I know you don't believe it. Stand back."

"Destroying me will only delay investigation. There are more like me," warns the Thing. And then says more pitiably, "Please do not destroy me."

"Back, gross mephitic beast," Chet says with a sense of dramatic relish. He raises his hands. "Here is an end to your monstrous and unhappy lies."

"Don't, Chet!" I yell, running and putting my arms out between them. "I want to know which of you is telling the truth. Stop! Just talk!"

"I am the one telling the truth, Christopher," says

the Thing, nodding its head erratically in my direction, trying still to keep an eye on Chet. "I am—"

"Come on, Christopher. Don't be stupid," says Chet. "There's nothing that the Forces of Darkness could do with the Arm of Moriator. The Arm destroys negative beings. That's why we activated it." He asks the Thing, "Can you explain that little inconsistency in your story?"

The Thing pauses. "We have not yet determined what use the Arm might be to you."

"No. I bet you haven't," says Chet. "You're not the—"

The Thing has raised its arms in some kind of spell.

Chet whacks his hands together. A blaze of light fills the room. My ears pound.

I lie flat on the floor.

The Thing bucks in agony, a latticework of veins ablaze on its skin, capillaries burning—it gapes terrified at its roasting hand—the suit melts into a blue polyester slurry—and from head to toe its skin peels away, an empty dirty husk, leaving nothing but a silver cord writhing like a worm on a griddle, seared with white light.

I cover my eyes from the glare.

There is a silence after the roar. In the vacuum, Paul's voice dribbles in informatively from the lawn. "This lumpy part is called the mantle. On either side of it, you can see two little holes as we pan in. These provide the breathing part of the slug, for the inhalation purposes of air and oxygen."

No one, I realize, has even heard the blast, any more than they could see the Thing. Carefully, I lift up my head. The wall-to-wall carpeting has made impressions on my face and arms.

Chet is standing there, on the bed, smiling inscrutably. The Thing is gone. "Do not fear, Christopher," Chet says. "I have defeated the foul fiend."

I get up on my knees and point at him. "Look," I say. "I don't know what's going on, but—"

"You could thank me for saving you. But it's all in a day's work. Well, time to go."

"No, Chet, wait! Wait!"

"I really have to go. Pressing business away West."

"Chet! If you want to prove yourself, cure me right now. Please. Then I'll believe you."

"Sorry, Christopher. No can do right now."

"Chet, I need help. I believe you, Chet."

"I'm glad you believe me, Christopher. That gives me a nice warm feeling deep down inside. I'll be back in a few weeks. Promise."

"Chet, damn it!"

"Hang tight 'til then."

"Chet!"

But he walks toward the wall, dissolving, shedding a gray cloud of atomized suit coat and flesh.

"Chet, damn it!"

He splashes into the wall and is gone.

It is as if he and the Thing had never been there.

My room is quiet. A bobbing green light from the sun and a tree outside swings like a yo-yo against the wall. Out in the yard, the peepers are chirping irregularly.

I can hear my brother's voice, muffled. "That dark stripe is the muscle, used for locomotion. Let's close in with the zoom lens and see what . . . ," he says. "Whoops. Eew. Eh! Ick! Shit! . . . Okay, end of take."


One day, the late spring rain is falling like marshmallow. Warm, wet, and sticky. The sickly pale green grass of spring is swamped with it. The gutters clog and clot with dirt and red wood chips.

My head is upside down like a bat, hanging off the end of the sofa. People in general don't like hanging upside down, but I can see why bats do it. It is not just the novelty of the way the blood in your head makes a sound like moths playing percussion. It is also great the way that you feel like you inhabit a different world. It's like people can't touch you, because they're aligned with the floor.

I am listening to my parents, and they seem farther away because they are in the right-side up world.

"Don't tell me that!" my mother is yelling. "Do you know how long it's been since you got a raise? Do you know?"

My father says something, but I can't hear it.

"What are you saying? Just tell me what you're

saying," screams my mother, "because I do everything I can to keep this family going, and I don't want to hear—"

My father says something else, very softly, but slams the table while he says it.

My mother says, "Your older son spends his life watching TV, your younger son—God knows—is doing drugs or—I don't even know what—and you're going out to play golf. Play golf! Great father! Golf! Go ahead, in the rain—I hope you get a bogey!"

Then they tell each other to go to hell, and they start slamming doors.

Upside down, everything seems so light and strange. The white lamp has risen like a bubble and now bobs against a tabletop. The *TV Guide* has shot up onto the sheltering sofa. Everything is poised with infinite care.

I have almost gone to sleep when my father comes in.

He says, "Christ," and walks out again. Then he looks in again. "What are you doing?" he demands. "Don't you have anything better to do than lie around daydreaming? You're not even right-side up. Get up. Do something."

So I get up. I start to pace.

As I pass through the front hall, my father is leaving to cool down in the car.

I pace in circles from room to room.

The first time around the house, I think about how I played right into the vampires' hands. I ask myself how

Chet could possibly use the Arm for evil. I do not come up with an answer.

The second time around the house (as I pass through the kitchen, where my mother is adding soap powder in the dishwasher), I think about how Chet would have come back and really helped me by now if he cared. If he were good, he wouldn't have abandoned me.

The third time around, I realize that I am all alone. I have probably played into the hands and claws of evil, and now I am all alone.

And my revolutions get quicker and quicker as I think: *Damn Chet, damn him because now I can't speak to anyone, can't tell anyone; and the thing I want to tell them most, the thing I need to say to them, is just that: that I can't speak, and that I'm all alone; and how can you tell people you're all alone when you're all alone?*

*How?*

Silence is there, stifling me like a dirty sock.

The afternoon rain drools down the gutters, and the birdseed washes around on the feeder dish. Rain muffles the house and drowns the yard.

My mother is sitting at the table, with her hands spread wide on the blond wood. The gray wet light of the rain has seeped into her hair and it is turning gray, too.

She looks up at me. She tilts her head to the side and moves it up so she is looking into my eyes. I stop my rotations. For a while, I stand there with my hand resting on the lintel of the kitchen door, looking into her eyes.

She looks very old and very human.

"Mom," I say tentatively. "Do you have a second?"

"I'm sorry about the fight," she says, blinking down, carefully slanting her fingers to match the grain of the wood. "Your father and I . . . can argue."

The rain is soft against the grass. "Do you . . . ?" I ask and hesitate. It is a dumb question. "Do you believe in angels? Not faeries or anything, but, you know, celestial beings sent to guide us?"

She looks at me longer. Then she looks down at her hands, which have pulled away from the wood of the table and curled fondly around each other. Then she stands and half sits on the table, with one heel resting against the bottom rung of a chair. She says to me, "I do. I guess I do." She frowns.

I move toward her. It is just about three steps. I am standing at the edge of the table nearest to her. Only a few inches away.

"In what way?" I say. "I mean, in that adult 'Yes, Virginia, there is a Santa Claus' way?"

She curls her lower lip uneasily beneath her upper teeth and shakes her head. "No," she says softly. "I think they are real."

"And that they intervene in human life?"

She raises her head and looks at me warily. "What do you mean?" she asks.

I stand there, my shoulders sloping, my hands at my sides. "I don't know," I admit.

With one hand she strokes the tabletop three times, and then she says, "I saw one once. I had . . . When I had . . . You were saved by one once." I wait for her to go on.

Finally, I say softly, so as not to disturb her, "How?"

The eaves are dripping. "When you were born," she says, "you were choking to death. That was . . . You were a breech birth, and somehow you got tangled up in the umbilical cord. We thought that . . . so—that it was all over."

The rain has let up a little. The dishwasher growls. I can hear Paul stomping upstairs. "Your face was blue. Really . . . I mean, blue. It . . . " She looks like she's about to cry. "A nurse came. She said, 'I'll take him. Just for a minute.' You were dead. You . . . She went into the next room."

Paul's radio goes on.

"Suddenly we heard this crying. It was you. She brought you in. She'd brought you back to life. It was . . . I mean, she was . . . It was a miracle. She brought you back." She has moved closer to me. And softly, urgently, she says, "And you're so wonderful, both you and Paul. We never could have imagined . . . I asked around, but no one knew who that nurse was. The room was full of people, but no one saw her come or go except your father and me." Her eyes are wet. "So, yes, I believe in angels."

"Chris, you're so special, and your father and I are so

concerned about you. We might fight, but you don't know how much we love you. Please, Chris," she says, shaking her head and pronouncing my name again and again as if each time she were caressing my hair. "Chris, Chris, Chris . . . "

She is so close, and I can tell she wants to take me in her arms like that baby she saw saved. Her upper body leans toward mine, and her hands have lifted off the table by several inches. Her face is pleading.

And I am standing so near to her, thinking of that small smiling family when I was saved from death, years before, and how they couldn't know what would happen, and how we all just want to be happy. I look at her, and I think we are both looking at each other and almost pleading for something with our eyes.

We stand there like that for a minute, sizing each other up to see who will embrace the other and show affection first, like sumo wrestlers crouching before the clinch.

And then suddenly I see it all—the other room, tangy with disinfectants, the nurse there in the dark, whatever they do to make you one—quickly chanting, or sprinkling me, or biting softly some hidden fold, some pudgy leg beneath the wrap—feeling my little dead toy heart quiver, thump with new life, thump again—how she smiled in the shadows, went out to greet the happy couple—cigars all around—

"Chris?" my mother says, leaning toward me. "Chris,

I love you," she says, sagging toward me, her face exhausted and in baboon folds. I twitch backward.

Quickly I say, "Yeah, well, I don't believe in them. I mean, I'm not sure. You never know."

Then I walk toward the door to the back hall where the washer and dryer, old welcome mat, and trash cans are. To my back she says, "Chris . . . ," and she says it so sadly that suddenly I feel like she is the child, a little girl; it hurts me to keep walking away. But I do.

And now she yells, "Chris. Christopher!"

As I go into the den, I hear her call, "Oh, fine! If you keep pacing, Christopher, if you pace one more god-damn time around this house, I swear I'm going to beat you until you can't sit down for a week."

So when I reach the front hall, I make a detour up the stairs to my room.

I lie on my bed with my head like a bat's.

The rain gets halfhearted as the evening falls. The evening is long and empty.

The yard is choked with water.


"Hello, Clayton police." Officer Melnikowski answers the phone. He came to our school to demonstrate school bus safety.

I say, "Hi. I'd like to report a vampire god trying to enter this world."

There's a silence on the other end of the phone.

"At the Sad Festival. I'm reporting that vampires are going to try to interrupt the spells to keep Tch'muchgar locked in another world."

Silence.

"He's going to try to break back into this world. And he'll wreak havoc and scatter destruction around him."

"Okay," says the policeman.

"They're meeting at an old abandoned church. You have to help me. I'm turning into a vampire, too. I can't give you my name yet."

"Slow down, slow down," he says. "This sounds serious."

"It is. You have to listen to me."

"Okay, okay. Calm. Right, I gotta ask you a couple questions."

"Go ahead," I say.

"First," he says. "Could you tell me: Is your refrigerator running?"

"This isn't a prank," I say.

"Second: Is this Mr. or Mrs. Wall? Well, if there aren't any walls there, how does the roof stay up?" I can hear laughing in the background. Those boys in blue.

"I am not kidding," I say angrily.

"No, and neither am I, kid. You call with this kinda sh—garbage again, I'll come over there and give you something to think about."

Then there's a dial tone.

I hang up angrily. It's a pay phone at school, because I don't want the police to trace the call back to me. I thought they might give me the benefit of the doubt. Obviously no help there.

"Hey," says Jerk, sauntering up. "Who you talking to?"

"I don't want to talk about it."

"Hey, okay, no problem." He puts his hands in his pockets and flexes his feet so he moves up and down. "You've been looking, like, really down recently."

"I'm sorry," I say, honestly sorry. "It's nothing to do with you."

"Would you like to come over after school and we'll, I don't know, play Kaverns of Kismet III or something?"

The idea stuns me with its worthlessness. I feel like I'm a million miles from Jerk.

So I apologize no, I'm going to the movies with my aunt. Jerk asks me which movie, sounding really interested, and I say I don't think we've picked one yet.

But even as I stand there lying to him, and as he realizes more and more that I'm lying, and gets quieter and sad around his mouth, I hate myself for saying these things. I make a silent pledge to be nicer to him, because even though he is a million miles from me, he wishes he weren't. Because there was a time when everything was simpler, and my friends were my friends.

Last year I got really excited about the lunchroom's Cajun sloppy joes. You would think that Cajun sloppy joes were not much to get excited about, but we live in a small town and not much happens some months.

Now I can't even eat our cook's Cajun sloppy joes. I'm sitting at the table, gagging just looking at one. Human food. Grease is rolling off the bun, and chunks of meat are quietly flopping down the sides and landing splayed in sauce, like ants dying of fumigation.

I can't put that thing in my mouth. It will be so pasty. But I'm so hungry.

I hate to feel my body out of control like this, to know that there's no way to just eat a normal thing and to be healthy. My body is changing—its sickness I don't understand, and its health is unhealthy—and I am constantly afraid because I don't know what will happen to me next.

Nearby, Tom is sitting with his crowd. I am sitting as close to them as I dare. As soon as I sit down, I realize how stupid it is. Rebecca is sitting a few seats away from me, but I feel like everything is falling apart, and I don't even know how I can think about stupid things like trying to impress her with witty lunch repartee when everything is sliding like it is.

She looks even more beautiful now that I know I'm falling apart. She's talking about the Cabala, an ancient book of mystical power she's studying with her uncle. Her friends are a little bit bored by her and keep poking their dessert squares. I love her for it. I could listen to her talk about the Cabala forever. If there were a CD called *Rebecca Schwartz Tells You About the Cabala*, for $14.99, I'd have three copies.

I am so swept up by Rebecca talking about the Cabala that I hardly even notice when I pick up the Cajun sloppy joe and take a big bite out of it like I would have done two months before. I hardly notice until the food is in my mouth, churning, sucking at my teeth as I gum it around.

Then I panic. It's sitting there on my tongue, evilly sitting on my tongue, like a fairy-tale toad on a lily pad. Lumpy. I can't breathe past it. My breath won't fit.

The room is suddenly very hot and crowded. My mouth is too full. There are people pushing and trays clacking, and an apple is flying through the air. My napkin is stained with red grease like blood.

My chair squeals backward and I run for the bathroom.

I push someone over. I say, "Sorry," but when I do, it all comes out: The lump of Cajun joe splats on the floor—and behind it, my breakfast. I'm heaving, and it's all there: orange juice, butter, home-style waffle.

Everyone is muttering and sniggering. Completely disgusted.

I'm supporting myself on one weak arm resting on a

tabletop. I raise up my head. Tom is looking at me like he's a total stranger who's just seen a murderer. I turn to the side because someone is running over with a mop and I realize that an umbilical cord of quivering spit still trails down to my pukey discharge.

I reach up grimly and, with a single finger, snap it.

I stand straight and tall and head for the men's room. My face is so hot it feels like my eyes must be red. I think it's embarrassment.

The janitor is arriving with the mop. I really want to offer to clean it up, but I can't. I don't even apologize to him. I just run for the bathrooms.

"Chris, wait up," I hear Jerk saying, back in the crowd. And then he says to someone else, "Man, I feel bad for him. He must be wicked sick."

The bathroom is white. That in itself is good. It feels as cool as a glacier. I splash cold water on my face. That's a mistake because I involuntarily snarl and start snapping at the water like a dog with a hose. Then I realize there's someone in one of the stalls, so I stop. Whoever he is, he pulls up his feet when he hears me growling.

I'm not in the mirror. I look, transfixed, at the tiles through my head.

I can't stay in here. No safety. Not with this bank of mirrors hollering out my vampirism like a Klaxon.

Got to get out of the building—that's all there is to it—until I can calm down.

I charge out of the bathroom and almost run into

Rebecca Schwartz, who's waiting by the bathroom door.

"Chris," she says. "I just came to see how you're doing."

"Fine," I say. "Fine."

"You looked really sick."

"I was," I say, backing up slightly. "I don't believe you came to see how I was doing! That's so nice. I've got to go."

"Hey," she says, reaching out to touch my elbow. "What's the problem? Everyone's wondering what happened."

I yank away from her touch. We're standing against lockers, gray metal lockers, on which I have no reflection. I keep my eyes glued to her face. She can't look down. Can't look at those lockers. I have to get away.

"I have to go," I say.

"You going home?" she asks.

"Yes," I say, shrugging. "I'll be back as soon as I've changed my name and grown a beard."

She laughs. "You just got sick," she says, "and yakked all over the floor." And then, more concerned, "Look, Chris, I, like, don't want to be a pain, but is everything okay? You've seemed really, you know, depressed and things recently. Throwing up can be a sign of nervousness. It was with my sister. She went through this whole depressed thing."

"No," I say. "I'm fine."

"Okay," she says. "It's just, I mean . . . Really, I don't

want you to think I'm being nosy or anything. But if you ever want to call someone and talk about it, you know you can call me. I mean, we had to deal with my sister and all."

I'm still not reflected in the lockers. Someone passes by, and Rebecca looks up at them. I take the opportunity to move a few inches away so I won't be so near the metal. She turns back and looks at me quizzically.

I splutter, "It's . . . mucus. I have all these springtime allergies, and I get all filled up with mucus. My stomach and things. All mucus."

She's smiling lightly. "Mucus? Are you sure? Not phlegm or sputum?"

"Mucus." I nod. "Yes."

"Okay. I'm serious, though, about calling me," she says. She goes to pat me on the arm.

I'm terrified her eyes will stray sideways. I stumble backward, yelp, "Bye!" and turn around and walk so fast that I'm almost running. I can feel her staring at me from behind, confused.

Later, I can't believe I didn't thank her more. Here she came forward and tried to help this big social pariah (i.e., me) and I didn't even thank her. I don't believe it.

I run home through the deserted factory, where no one will be looking for me in car window reflections, or in plate glass windows. I run home and lie on my bed until the danger is past, and I am once again in mirrors.

That night, I cannot sleep.

I stare groggily at the ceiling, and I can hear their pulses. It is probably my imagination, but I think I can hear my family's pulses spread throughout the house. A matrix of tiny pulses throughout the house, like the movements of mice. I lie there in what should be silence, hearing each different heart kick in contraction. And again. Again. Again.

I lie awake and listen to the clattering of hearts, this festival of cardiac bongos to which I'm not invited. I can hear them through the plasterboard.

I've got to see if it is me hallucinating.

I get up. I open the door to the hallway.

I pause for a moment with my hands resting on the sides of the door frame. A thin breeze crawls up the shapeless, grimy T-shirt I wore to bed and pats my belly.

I can feel their heartbeats all around me. My brother in his bedroom, my mother in her king-size bed, my father tonight in the guest bed, each room with its own distinctive beat.

I choose my brother's room. His pulse is youngest.

I pad over, my feet soft against the carpet.

The knob grates as it turns, but I am so careful it is not loud. The tongue of the door clasp retracts like the end of a kiss, and the door swings wide.

Of course, I am not going to do anything. I am just

going to prove to myself that I am only hallucinating, that I cannot honestly hear those pulses. That is all I am going to do.

I slip in. I close the door behind me. I will just check.

A few stripes of streetlamp light from between the slatted blinds run across Paul's rumpled bed. I take two paces forward.

Silence. Nothing but silence and the passing of a car outside on the street and a high whine of fear in my own head.

It was nothing. Half-sleep. Wishful thinking. A frantic dream. Now there is no heartbeat.

I step to the edge of the bed. To take a closer look. He is tangled in his covers. One gross hairy leg juts out. A hand-held video game is half-trapped under his pillow.

I reach out slowly to touch his neck. I can see his throat flexing with each breath.

*Why am I doing this?* I ask myself in panic.

I step closer to him. His neck flexes as he turns away, muscles rippling across the surface. He has a mole on his neck. Like a target.

Blood. I can feel the blood skating through his skin, dashing like light on water. The liveliness of mortal flesh.

I lean toward him. Just to take a closer look.

I can almost touch his neck with my tongue.

I crouch there.

Panicked.

His mouth is open idiotically. A slug's trail of drool leads onto his pillow.

I move my hands up to my mouth.

Cover it. Both hands.

Start backing up. Like a broken wind-up toy. Step by step. Toward the door.

Carefully undo the latch.

Go back to my room.

For a while, I just sag there against my bed, breathing raggedly.

He is still just a room away.

I was not going to do anything. Nothing like that. I just went in to check if the pulses were real. They were a dream. That's it. I just wanted to check about the pulses, though.

That was it

On the wall there is a portrait of someone with no skin. They still look like they're smiling for the artist, but that may be because they have no cheeks.

The doctor is pulling my records. That's what he told me, at least. "Wait just a sec. Let me pull your records." So I am sitting in a backless tunic with my bare butt on the paper of the table, swinging my legs, and I've read most of the April issue of *Highlights for Children*

The doctor comes in again.

"Feeling chilly?" he says.

"I have no pants on," I reply.

"That's true," he says. "You don't like the tunic?"

"I feel like I'm dressed for a science fiction film," I say. "Maybe this is why the *Star Trek* team always beams up with their backs to the wall."

He stares at me, frowning, and sits down. He opens the file. For a long time, he looks over the file.

The doctor looks up. "I've asked for your dental records to be faxed over from Dr. Shenko's office."

"I had a bad accident," I explain.

The doctor regards me coldly.

"I ran into a large object. And hurt myself."

"Chris," he says, "you know your parents are very concerned. They say you're not sleeping much and you've become very different to them."

I'm starting to feel uncomfortable.

He continues, "They say you've seemed very tired and cranky recently."

"It's just a phase," I say. I'm hoping to fool him. "I was wondering if I could have some advice about what to do with my hormones and things. The confusing changes that are going on in my body."

"Chris." He sizes me up. He is looking at me and wondering something. I don't know what. "Chris, has anyone approached you recently and said anything strange to you? Touched you in an unusual way?"

I stare back at him. I've got to move carefully. "No. Are you saying . . . ? No, I mean, I don't think so."

"Do you wear any religious symbols about your person?"

"No," I answer. "I had a cross, but I lost it swimming."

"Please think. Has anyone spoken to you recently in a language that did not seem human? Made passes in the air near your body with their hands or any kind of unusual prop? Has anyone bitten you, Christopher? Not even just on the neck. These are all avenues of inquiry I'd like to explore."

"No. None of those."

"Has anything happened recently that you'd like to tell me about?" He looks almost like he's sneering. I can't calculate what's going on in his head, because I can't tell what he's like as a person. I try wildly to picture him at a cookout. I figure, if I can just picture him at a cookout, how he would smile and wave to people on a lawn and whether he would offer to work the grill, I can figure out what makes him tick, and I can give him the right answers.

I shrug. "No. What kinds of things?"

He's just looking at me. I feel very thin and naked and realize how awkward I am hunched over on the table with my ugly feet dangling and a copy of *Highlights for Children* on my lap, open to Goofus and Gallant.

He rolls his chair closer. He leans in toward me. Like a threat, he says in a whisper, "If anything—*anything*—strange . . . If anything strange happens to you." As he whispers low, one hand makes a sawing motion across the other. "If the slightest urge . . . If you have the slightest urge that you think might be unusual or unnatural . . . If that should happen, I want you to call me immediately. We'll come and pick you up. Do you understand, Christopher? You won't be hurt. It's for your own good. For your own good."

I'm looking at his hands. His voice says, "Do you understand? For your own good." But his hand is sawing, and sawing, and sawing away at his fingers.

It is one week to the Sad Festival of Vampires.

In the city of Worcester, which is partially serviced by our reservoir, one day the water is turned to blood. There is no water anywhere in the northern part of the city. Faucets spit blood. Blood spatters out of spigots, splashes out of hoses to stain the bushes dark; gore begrimes stacks of greasy plates and shoots out of drinking fountains to make people gag.

Torrents of blood flow down drains and stain the gutters.

There are screams as it happens. People sobbing hysterically and grinding their bloody hands in dishtowels. People throwing up in restaurants. Sorcerers and psychics saying that it is a sign from God, an alien invasion, the anger of the Little People. I wish I could have been in Worcester.

It lasts for only an hour. Then sweet water flows. But by then, the damage is done.

The blood has clotted in the pipelines. Scabs five miles long.

Now I am sure. Chet is not coming. Tch'muchgar is coming. He is feeling his way into this world, preparing himself for the leap.

There is not much time left.


Darkness.

Down the street I walk. The streetlights are buzzing.

It is a hot night. People are cooped up in their houses. They are asleep, and I wonder if, even in sleep, they can tell they're cooped up, like zoo animals roused when they roll over against the bars.

I have to talk. I have to.

Rebecca Schwartz. Three o'clock is probably too late to drop by and shoot the breeze. But it is a warm night, and the thick leaves are restive and suggest to me that all the night is alive and I should be reveling in it.

If Rebecca were a vampire, if she were damned, we could be together. This is not a serious thought, but I think it anyway, how it would be for us to be together. We live in a high dark house in the woods; our walls hung with incomprehensible pieces of modern art by the friends we have and must leave when they notice that age does not wither us. At night, we stalk the grounds and lie together by the ebony fountain clogged with amber leaves. Sometimes we cry whole ages of darkness together because of our common sin, but there is no one else to whom we can turn, and so we understand each other completely. We know each strange motion that the other makes and what it means. As the eons pass, we come to be very genteel, and I am more suited to her and not so awkward all the time, and after a few centuries my athlete's foot clears up.

That all seems to make so much sense that I want to go speak to her now, and it takes me a moment to remember that I hardly even know her. That she would stare at me, aghast; that if she knew, she'd hate me and run inside and lock the door. That she is not my chilly queen of the night. That she wears jeans and loses her hair clips.

Tom I think about only briefly. I can't trust him.

So I head to Jerk's. Jerk may be Jerk, but he is the one person who is always loyal. He will always be loyal to me. I need to tell him and have him say that there's something we can do.

After a while, I reach his house. The lights are all off. There are bleached sand toys scattered around the front lawn. There's a wading pool with the hose dangling in it. I start to cross the lawn.

There's a low growl.

I look around, breathing the air in deeply. I see shrubs and a tree and the aluminum siding. Jerk's room is on the ground floor, but the window is around the back. The snarl comes again.

A dog is slinking toward me, growling like a crazy jackal.

"Bongo," I hiss. "Bongo."

He stops and shivers.

I look into his eyes.

I am so thirsty and so tired of all this. I'm tired of all this sneaking around and endless complaining. I want the damn dog to get out of the way.

Carefully, I step toward it with my hands stretched out.

I find it cannot move. "Bongo," I repeat, quietly but coldly, almost like a warning. "Bongo. Bongo."

I take another step forward.

My hand shoots out and fastens on its head.

My thumb and pinkie slip down either side of its neck. I can feel the dog's pulse. I can feel the warmth of its blood. Its eyes are going wacko, shooting around looking for an escape. But its body can't move. My eyes are fixed on it. I know that if, for one second, I stop staring at it, it will start barking.

My saliva is running fast and thick. I can barely keep it in my mouth. I can feel this dog like a drink. Carefully, I rotate the head up. It tries to stop me, but my strength, I find, is great. I rotate the snout up by eighty degrees, until the dog is looking almost straight up. It is gulping with fear. I can see its throat flexing. I move my other hand, almost lovingly, to the soft down below its neck.

Pushing the head up a few more degrees, I encounter the resistance of bone. The head will twist only a few more degrees before things start to pop and snap.

I lower my head, drooling.

Good-bye, Bongo, I think sardonically.

My heart beats faster.

I nuzzle the soft fur with my lips. Open my jaws.

I am ready to kill him.

But then I think of that name . . .

Bongo. Bongo the dog.

Jerk must have named him, years ago, when he was little. When Jerk was just a little Jerk, his parents' hope and joy and all, saying, "Lesss call him *Bongo*. The puppy. *Bongo*."

And I think about Jerk finding the corpse, drained and twisted. And I must remain human. I can't believe what I want to do.

I will remain human at any cost. I drop the dog.

The second I let go, Bongo is barking like mad. I run, but he's chasing me, and barking, and now I really don't know what I'm going to do.

The road is slapping under my feet, and I'm heading down under the streetlamps.

He stands barking, barking, barking at me under a stop sign, as if that were the speech balloon translation.

But I run on, through the suburbs. I run past the

funeral home and its lawns, under the sagging power lines, past the darkened windows of the twenty-two-hour convenience store. I run under the railroad bridge.

I am going to search the woods for a raccoon or something. I am not cold, and I do not mind the company of twisted trees and haunted bracken. I am doing the haunting now.

I have to keep spitting because my saliva is so thick and choking. I really want to kill, and I think how people like Tom would be surprised because they don't think of me as very wild or savage or strong.

I envision the raccoon's death: I see my shirt torn from the little claws; I rip it off, yanking my way down the row of buttons. I see myself sucking on the carcass, on the thick sweet blood, and it runs down my wrists to my bare chest and drips on my belly, mingling with my own blood, and I smear the skin over my own skin.

And in my vision, I stand in the dawn in the devil's orchard by the water tower, watching the sun rise over the reservoir, full of life, the blood caking warmly on my pale skin as the three radio towers blink and blurt out their silent soft rock like gagged victims bleating for help. The sun throws sludgy scarlet smudges over the morning clouds. The trees are full of life; and in the dawn, they are ruby like gore.

That is my vision.

But I find no raccoons.

I look for hours. Nothing. Trees

I walk for the rest of the night. A light drizzle falls as morning approaches. All the while, I am thinking that I will never be the same again—that's the terrifying thing—that Chet will not come, and that I will never be the same again, and that I will be condemned to endless wandering, wandering through tiny towns and lying down in alleys in big cities, lying drunk or in wait of victims, forgetting that I grew up at all, forgetting this life of green avenues and my brother's dumb swears and my mother's voice and my father's quiet love of golf.

Chet will not come, and I will have to flee. They will chase me. The crowd will want to kill me.

I think of Tom—untrustworthy, eyes narrow—and of my father—mute and nervous—and my mother—"It wasn't even human"—about the changeling child on TV—"It wasn't even human"—

And a voice says to me again and again this one chilling fact I know is true: that I came into this world from a warm place within someone else; but that I will leave it completely alone.

I walk through the woods until I come again to the road. I start home. My shirt is intact.

I am a failure, even as a vampire.

*alienation / isolation*

When I reach my house, it is dawn. My mother is waiting for me in the kitchen. She's dressed in a pink bathrobe, but it looks gray in the dawn. Everything in

*existential angst*

the kitchen looks gray: the table looks gray, and the dish-washer, and the sink, and my mother, too, who is in a chair.

"Where have you been?" she barks at once, suspiciously. "Where the hell have you been? *Where?*" She hits the table. "Where the *hell* have you been?"

I have to make up an excuse, but the sun is coming up and I'm suddenly very, very tired. I've been out almost all night, since midnight. "I just went out, just now, to, um," I explain groggily, "check the tree."

It is admittedly not the best or most coherent lie I have ever made up.

I shuffle past her toward the front hallway.

"Christopher! Stop, Christopher," she says, but this time softer, as if she's scared to know the answer. "You've been at a party, haven't you? Have you been out at a party?"

I know she doesn't want to hear. I can tell she's afraid.

So I don't answer and go upstairs.

I sit down on my chair. I lay my head down on my desk like it's a broken appliance and I'm dropping it off for repairs.

Briefly, I sleep. I dream of wielding great gouts of fire that wallop the vampires, as they cast their wicked spells. I dream of being cured by a kind touch from Chet. I dream that Rebecca Schwartz loves me and I talk to her like I would talk to no one else. I picture her careful, clever face, and I picture kissing it and her smooth white neck. I kiss her right where the pulse is, and I can feel how hot her blood is. I can feel it moving through her like quick fire; I can sense it caressing her breasts from the inside, circling like electrons around her secret womb.

I can feel it in my mouth, running down my throat. I feel strong again; I feel alive; I feel the spark of her life twitching in my heart as she drains into me, from under me, as I feel her spasms beneath me and her death.

My alarm rings. A half hour has passed. It is time for school. I lift my head slowly, like a moss-covered prehistoric sea turtle might if it were woken up by B movie radiation leakage.

Even the early morning sun is painful. I stand up.

I am not a morning person.

I am not an afternoon person either.

I guess that I am not a person at all.

# CHAPTER 7

It is the Sad Festival of Vampires.

At midnight, the runes and spells of warding will have been read, the White Hen shut, and the fate of the world decided.

And if Tch'muchgar is to come from his prison world and thunder through the forests he will have come; and there will be screaming in the lonely houses by the lake and burning in the towns.

And I do not know what to do.

Every city has its rituals to stave off evil and to satisfy the Forces of Light. At least in Clayton, we don't sacrifice people anymore. In Boston it is bad because every year virgins must be offered to the spirits there.

There it is done democratically, through a lottery. The night before the lottery, the city holds a great celebration, like Mardi Gras. Originally, it was a night when families could be together for maybe the last time before the name was drawn, the name of a virgin daughter or son. Now it is a difficult night for parents; they must decide whether to enjoy that last night together, sitting sadly in party frocks around their dining room table while outside the horns razz and glass breaks, or whether to push their sons and daughters out of the house, out into the parties and sweat, and tell them to go and lose their virginity in the crowds.

Needless to say, the night before the lottery is held each year, many seniors from our school take the Worcester-Boston bus, whooping and pounding on the windows. The next morning they come back out in the dismal light with stories of what they did behind dumpsters or in hotels.

Nobody knows what happens to the sacrifices after they're left in a vault beneath the city. Usually they're just gone in the morning and are never heard from again. Once, a mangled and tattered body was seen cawing and flapping its way crowlike out to sea.

In any case, in Clayton our rituals are not so dramatic.

From the *Clayton Crier*:

> I've heard spring's over and summer's here—a little bird told me! School's almost out and the nights are getting hot. And that means only one thing: time for the Wompanoag Valley Sad Festival of Vampires!
>
> Yes, step right up, step right up for the best weekend of singing and dancing and carnival rides you'll ever sink your teeth into! The fair is coming to Barley's Field! That means fun, hayrides,

clowns, games, carbonation, whipped cream, sacrificial goats in the petting zoo, etc., etc.! And while you're there at the fair on Saturday night, from nine to midnight catch the loudspeaker broadcast of our quaint and ancient ritual of binding the Vampire Lord! So come: Listen, eat, drink, and be merry!

Sad Festival? It should be called the Happy Festival!

—by Cheryl Paluski

It has begun.

This is the night of tears; the time of fear; sorrow abiding at the eventide.

Paul and his friend Mark and I are driving to McDonald's. They have a special there in which you can buy two Big Macs for two dollars.

My mother sent me out with Paul. He's going to the big party Tony and Kathy Rigozzi have every year. Tony is Paul's age. I think Kathy is in college by now. They live right next to Barley's Field, where the carnival is, and my mother wants me to go to the carnival. She says my friends will be there. She says that I don't see my friends much anymore. She's worried about me. I don't have the heart to tell her I don't have friends anymore.

"I've heard this party is great," says Mark, sliding his

hand up and down the shoulder strap. "I mean, I've heard that sometimes girls dance with no top on . . ."

"No way," says Paul.

"Yeah way."

"No goddamn way."

"*Yeah* way."

"No way, you meat-brained monkey-licker."

"What?!?" asks Mark, laughing. "What's that, like, supposed to *mean?*"

Paul squeals, "How should I know, ear-sucking skunk-tart?"

"Welcome to McDonald's. May I take your order?"

Across the parking lot, there are three girls silhouetted against the streetlights. And I see one has the aura around her, the double shadow. She is slim and beautiful with taut, tan legs. But she is not human. She has the darkness of vampirism all about her.

And I realize: *To her, I will have an aura, too.*

They are looking this way. I have to hide.

Paul calls into the night, "One double Big Mac Super-Huge Value Pack . . ."

"One for me, too," Mark whispers.

"Make that two. Two double Big Mac Super-Huge Value Packs." Paul turns to me. "Buttplug?"

But—like a rabbit in headlights—"I don't . . ."

"What?" Paul waits. "What do you want?"

I've panicked. That's it—I jump to the floor. Curl up. Below the level of the windows.

"Chris?" says Paul.

I'm looking down. I'm looking at the upholstery of the car and the rugs. The rugs are littered with crumbs. The back of the driver's seat has split slightly, and white foam is pressing outward at the dirty seam, like spittle round a madman's smile.

"I don't know," I repeat, babbling. "I don't know, I don't know, I don't know."

Mark looks at me. "Something wrong?"

Paul is saying, "This isn't a difficult one, Chris."

"No," says Mark to Paul, seriously. "Turn around. Look at him."

Paul shifts around in his seat. He asks me more carefully, "Hey, what's wrong, man?"

"I don't know. I don't know. Don't look at me. Turn around. McNuggets. Fries. A . . . I don't know."

Mark and Paul look at each other. Paul shrugs.

Mark asks, "Do you think he wants an apple pie?"

Paul searches my eyes, confused, and turns back to the speaker. "I guess a nine-piece Nuggets, large fries . . . You want a drink?"

He waits, facing forward, his eyes creeping around to look at me.

"Medium Coke," he says finally.

"That comes to $12.26. Please proceed to the second window."

"Do you want to go home?" asks Paul. We prowl forward around the topiary Grimace.

"Is that Jenny Morturo?" asks Mark urgently, ducking and pointing behind us. "Wonder if she's going."

"Whoo! Woah, boy!" says Paul, and they give each other five.

Mark is waving like a man on an ice floe meeting an ocean liner.

Jenny Morturo has tumbled dark hair and deep, deep red lipstick. She leans against her car. She waves once, then saunters over. Mark rolls down the window—he gets it wrong at first and starts rolling it up.

The other two—another girl and the vampiress—follow Jenny toward us.

"Hi, Jenny," Mark says.

"Hey. How you doing?" drawls Jenny.

"I'm doing well."

"We're 'well,' too," says Jenny Morturo, smiling. "That's Mark and Paul," Jenny tells her friends. "They're 'well.' This is Ashley."

"Nice to meet you. I'm Mark."

"Hi, Mark. I'm Ashley. Spelled A-S-H-E-L-E-I-G-H-E."

"Hi. I'm Paul. Spelled. You know."

"And this is Lolli."

"Nice to meet you, Lolli."

"And you, Mark." (Lolli nods.) "Paul; Christopher."

No one has told her my name.

Paul laughs uneasily. He says, "My younger brother does not usually lie curled up in, you know, the fetal position on the floor of my car."

Jenny is making a face. "Is he . . ." She taps her fragrant, unruly chestnut curls.

"No," says Paul. "Just tonight."

"Are you going to this party?" Lolli asks. "I've just been invited."

"We sure are," says Mark. "You?"

"We'll follow you," says Jenny.

Lolli taps on my window. I can see the glare of her claw-red nail polish in the streetlights. "Please don't feed the animals," she jokes.

"Is he, like, okay?" says Asheleighe. "He looks, like, très weirdamundo stressed."

"He'll uncurl as the night goes on," Lolli prophesizes.

Jenny has backed up and slips her key ring over one pronged finger; as she draws it over her stiffened knuckle she says, "You lead. We'll be right behind you."

I watch Lolli Chasuble walk away. Everything about her seems alert and cunning. I can tell how those eyebrows, dark and sure, would arch and work as she sucked on someone's neck. She has made up her face as carefully and with as much malice as a warrior arraying himself for battle.

I am frankly afraid of her.

Mark is rolling up his window. "This is great," he announces. "This is so great."

Paul is heaving in his seatbelt to try to fit his wallet back into his pocket. "Yessiree Bob," he says. "But just keep hold, man."

"Keep hold? This is going to be the greatest party ever!"

"Keep hold."

"I can't believe this!"

"Keep hold! Report to mission control, man!"

"Capsule to mission control."

"Read you, capsule man."

"Stardate 3867.5. Ready to blast off. Orders?"

"Lock phasers . . . to stun."

"A-OK!"

"Warp five, Mr. Sulu."

And we pull out of the drive-thru.

The three girls are in their car and they drive close behind Paul. At the stoplight, Jenny pulls her car up hard behind ours and nuzzles our bumper.

"She is wild," says Paul to Mark.

"She is," says Mark, nodding. "Wild."

We drive out through the forests and fields. As Jenny's car kisses ours, Paul says, "Tell her it's getting a little rough."

Mark nods and rolls down the window. Our heads jerk as Jenny bumps us again and flashes her high beams. "Thank you!" Mark calls back, his black hair flopping. "Thank you, that will be enough."

I am curled up in the back seat. I don't want to be caught in the harsh-seeing glare of those headlights.

I collapse onto the floor at another impact.

"Damn, man," says Paul. "What's the big idea? Can you tell them to—"

"Let me off at the fairground," I say suddenly. I have to avoid her. "Before we get to the Rigozzis'. Let me off at the fairground."

"Okay, fart-cheese. Whatever you say. You going to be all right?"

"Yes," I say. "Tom and Jerk will be there. Everything will be hunky-dory."

We are hurtling through the carnival night.

I picture talking to Rebecca Schwartz. It is a stupid fantasy. I picture saying, "I am a vampire now, but with you I can save the world." We are at the fair, and the lights swing in ballet around us to the music of the merry-go-round.

Then someone will understand. Then someone will take me in her arms. She will kiss me, and we will run to the police. We will bang on desks. We will shout. We will stand by and watch as the helicopters, their tails like wasps' low with poison, buzz over the knotted forests, spraying the dark and enchanted places with gallons and gallons of holy water.

That is my dream.

I do not know what to do.

I do not know at all.

"There's Chris!" says Jerk, looking up from a big unwieldy scab of fried dough and a game called "Shoot Like the Pros."

Tom is standing, his back against the booth, arms folded, looking around with quick catlike motions for some people who are his friends.

"Hey, Chris," Jerk says, running forward. "This a great carnie, or what?"

I feel strangely sorry for him, but I still find myself saying flatly, "Oh boy, oh boy. What a great time."

Tom has decided to walk toward me. He does it in a way that suggests that moving five steps in my direction is an early birthday present. "Hey," he says. "How did you get here?"

"Paul drove me. He's going to the Rigozzis'."

"The Rigozzis' *party*?" exclaims Jerk.

"Like everyone else," says Tom. "Everyone goes to that party."

"It's supposed to be really cool," says Jerk.

Tom nods. "I heard that last time all these girls danced topless."

"No," says Jerk. "Like who?"

"Jane McKinley, Liz Dinn . . ."

"No. Like, no way."

"Besta Worritz . . ."

There are three girls, all leaning into one another's shoulders, tripping along and laughing, and one of them has dangling from her arm a big pink fuzzy gecko that she has won; I look carefully at her freckles, for they are soft, and brown, and dashed across her face like cinnamon across a fine dessert. Suddenly my throat constricts, and I feel the beginnings of the thirst coming on. I can tell it will come on strong as the night goes on.

Tom looks boldly into my eyes. "So can you get us in?"

"No," I say. "Just, my brother is there."

"Come on. It'll be great. There is going to be, like, all this major action there."

"No," I say. "There's someone I don't want to see there. A girl."

Tom looks at Jerk. "I'm going to go anyway. So many people there, they aren't going to notice one more."

"Yeah, great!" says Jerk, smiling. "Or two more!"

"Okay," says Tom. "You can come. Just don't act like a complete dorkus totalus and embarrass me—got it?" He starts walking toward the Rigozzis' house. "You coming?" he asks me.

People are howling in the bouncy castle of fun.

"No," I say quietly. "I'm not."

Tom doesn't even acknowledge I've spoken. He just turns his back and starts walking. Jerk stumbles to catch up to him, but keeps looking back over his shoulder, just to see if I've changed my mind.

I am thinking hard. I am trying not to panic. *Why is she here?* I am wondering. *Why?* She must be here for me. She is supposed to take me to the abandoned church. I bet that's it. Otherwise there is no really obvious reason for an undead being to attend the Bradford/Clayton Carnival. It is $1.50 for just a small

7-Up. She wishes to take me to the convocation of vampires for her own dark purposes.

And that is when I realize that perhaps it would be the best thing.

I don't know what I'm going to do. I have started something by dropping that disk into darkness, and I don't know what. I have played into Chet's hands, and I don't know how. But I do know that I am helpless while I'm stranded here at the carnival.

So that is what I need to do, I realize suddenly. I will go with her. I will let Lolli Chasuble take me to the hidden coven of vampires again. The wizards and sorcerers of that vampire band will be locked in their vicious ceremony, trying to interrupt the festival spells being cast on the lake. At the height of the vampires' spells, right when the bonds are about to break, when the tension is greatest, right before Tch'muchgar hurtles back into this world through whatever convoluted means Chet may have worked out, I'll throw myself into the center of them, call out the Lord's Prayer, obscure their runes, gash the high sorcerer's face with my keys, anything to botch their spells of summoning, anything to break its stranglehold, to let the festival rites be spoken.

The vampires will kill me after that. I don't have any doubt that they will. But there is nothing else I can do.

So I will find Lolli Chasuble after all. I will have to face her sometime.

And with that, I run after Jerk and Tom. I follow their

backs until I've caught up to them, grim and puffing.

I say, "I'm coming after all."

"Great!" says Jerk.

"Let's go," says Tom.

We head toward the Rigozzis' party.

Over the scream of people on Captain Hook's Giddy Galleon, there is a sound of broadcasted voices. "Testing," it says across the uneven grass, the crowds, and the litter of ticket stubs and crushed cups. "Testing."

"They're going to start the ritual," says Jerk. "Cool."

"I'm so glad you could all make it this evening," the speakers say. "I'd like to thank everyone who made tonight's ritual sacrifice possible and, of course, everyone involved in the committee that organized this wonderful festival, which is really great this year. Great festival! Isn't it great? I'd like to thank them all."

Our mayor is addressing us. We're walking. I am picturing finding Rebecca Schwartz and talking to her, explaining myself, before I go off on my date with the daughter of the damned. There is a touching scene where Rebecca is crying at my funeral. It would be great if I could speak to her before I go.

One person needs to know of the sacrifice I'm about to make.

We pass the tilt-a-whirl. People in neon teacups are being flung out over the sweet cow-cropped grass; they're giggling; boys are trying to lean and spin their cups; girls are screaming "No! No!"

"Father Bread," says the mayor over the loudspeakers. "Would you do the honors?"

"Thank you, Mayor," says Father Bread. He adds, "Ehhrm," rattling as he takes the microphone. Then he begins, echoing out over the booths and the fields and the hot summery oaks, "We call upon the great hierarchy of angels for their aid in the shadows of night."

The beginning of the spell of binding. That means nine o'clock. Three hours for me to find the convocation of vampires and do something to stop them.

I'm in a sweat.

The Rigozzis live on the edge of Barley's Field in a big green Colonial house with a three-car Colonial garage. People are wandering out of the house over to the carnival and back again. Music pounds inside the house.

"Time to crash, boys!" says Tom.

"I feel bad about crashing," I say. "What if they find out?"

"Your brother is in there."

I say uneasily, "I'd really rather wait for an invitation."

"God you're impossible," says Tom. "Come on," he says to Jerk and walks up the steps.

"I'll wait out here for a minute with Chris," says Jerk. "Couldn't we find Tony Rigozzi and ask him?"

"Christ!" says Tom. He walks up the three concrete steps to the front door. He opens the door. Inside there is music and dancing. He hesitates, just for one moment, and moves his lips together nervously. Then he walks in.

He slams the door behind him.

"Hey, bruiser," says a voice from behind one of the bushes at the front door. "Waiting for an invitation?"

The bush waggles, and out into the light steps a young man with messy blond hair, an armless jean jacket, and a bat tattooed on his arm. "Chris, good to see you. We thought you'd come around," he says. "Bat is my name, and it is my symbol. The bat. I move by night and seek things out by screaming."

Jerk isn't very comfortable. He doesn't like Bat much.

And I see that Bat has an aura. He is a vampire. I remember the tattoo. I saw him before at that abandoned church, where he ate the flesh of women in casseroles.

He says, "Lolli Chaz is looking forward to seeing you." And, "She has quite an evening planned for you. Come on, sucker."

He walks up the three concrete steps to the front door. He wipes his feet on the welcome mat and swings the door open.

"Heya heya heya!" he screams. "Someone gonna invite me *in*, man?"

There's a momentary pause inside. I can't see past Bat. In a second, Tony Rigozzi, a junior at my school, stumbles over to the door, laughing, spilling beer from a plastic cup. "Whoa! My first day," he says, "with my goddamn *new legs*."

"Friend of Lolli Chasuble," says Bat. "Can I come in?"

Tony laughs again. "Shit, yes! Everyone's invited! What're you waiting for, a . . . ? Get in there! My house is your house. It is! It's your goddamn house!"

"Great, man," says Bat, punching Tony on the upper arm. "I'm damn glad to meet you."

"That a real tattoo?" says Tony, stubbing his fingers on Bat's upper arm. "Man, that real?"

"No," says Bat, secretly motioning to me with his other arm. "Got it out of a box of *goddamn Cracker Jack*!"

I walk up the steps with Jerk. We're lingering right behind Bat.

"Lolli's over there," says Tony, waving his hand toward the living room. "Dancing on the table. She's some . . ." He sizes Bat up. "So, you her boyfriend?"

"No," says Bat.

"No? She is something," Tony says in an undertone "I mean, look at her."

"She's nice," murmurs Bat.

They're standing close, side by side now, needling each other in the ribs. Tony says, "Those lips were made for more than talking, huh?"

Bat smirks, says, "Heh heh heh."

And they disappear into the living room.

The door is left open.

"We could go back to the carnie if you wanted," says Jerk. "The, like, haunted house is only seventy-five cents. I mean, I've been in it four times, but there's a really good skeleton and stuff."

I shake my head. "No. I've got to go in. Come if you'd like. Or go. It's up to you."

I snap my fingers from nervousness. Then I go in to find her.

The party is in full swing. People are packed up and down the front stairs right near the door. They're leaning on the dining room table and dancing in the living room. Kids are singing with the music, playing air guitar, slam dancing delicately, and gargling beer.

Lolli whirls like an Indian goddess of destruction atop a side table, scattering issues of *Good Housekeeping* with her heels. She and Jenny are dancing, pointing at each other, casting their shoulders back and forth, up and down.

Lolli's friend Asheleighe is perched on the arm of the sofa, yelling over the music to Trunk McIntyre, "I, like, loved their first album totally, but then when their second album came out, it was like, god, way to be completely queer, all right?"

Trunk nods. After some thought, he washes the beer from one cheek to the other and swallows. He says, "Yeah!"

I pass Paul. He has waylaid Tony, blathering, "Hey, Tony, Tony, I was thinking. I brought my camcorder.

It's out in the car. I was thinking, like, I could—"

"Yeah, great, man," says Tony.

"No, Tony, I could bring it in and we could make a movie. You know, it would be fun, we'd preserve this party for future generations unseen? Do some crazy video stuff?"

"Yeah, whatever, guy," says Tony. "My house is your house." He turns and calls, "Chester *boy*! I see you *standin'* there, but I don't see you *guzzlin'*!"

I look around and spot Tom standing on the other side of the room, talking with some other people from the cooler crowd in our class. One of them is Rebecca.

I work my way through the crowd.

"Hi, Chris," Chuck, Andy, Kristen, and Rebecca say when I join them. We're all a couple years younger and more timid than everyone else at the party, so I'm on their level for a few minutes. Tom sees that they've said hello to me, then he says hi, too, as if we're just meeting up.

"Great party," says Chuck. "That girl Lolli, who's dancing with Jenny Morturo, she says she knows you."

"Yes," I say.

"You know *her*?" Tom asks, somewhat in awe. She bucks her shiny pelvis; her tan legs kick.

"Yes," I repeat.

"From where?" says Andy.

"Around," I say.

Jerk has come up and stood next to us, peering at Tom and Kristen and Andy as if he were one of their crowd, but he is too shy to say hello. Rebecca says hi to him anyway—"Hi, Jerk"—which I think is nice. She gives him a quick smile.

So we're standing there.

Time is running out. I feel anxious to begin, to talk to Lolli, to get on the road, to find the abandoned church again. Maybe two hours and forty-five minutes left until midnight, and the final part of the Spell of Binding is cast. Rebecca first, though. She has to know. I have to tell her.

"Rebecca?" I say. Feeling weak, I look deep into her feet. "I was wondering, I mean . . . Could . . . ?"

Everyone waits. Tom is raising his eyebrows.

"Could I talk to you for a minute?"

"Whoa whoa whoa!" says Chuck. "Looks like you've got yourself an admirer!" he says to Rebecca.

Andy and Chuck laugh. Tom doesn't know whether he's supposed to laugh or not.

I say, "You can—" And then I feel Lolli's soft arms wrap up around my shoulders from behind, like she's about to do the Heimlich maneuver.

"Hi there, Chris," she says. "Saw you from over there and thought you might like to step upstairs for a little talk."

Chuck and Andy back off a step. They are blinking. Chuck whispers, "Shit . . ." Jealously.

Rebecca is obviously disgusted. She's looking at Kristen.

I say, "Lolli, you. I mean, I need to talk to you, too, but first I want to talk, I mean, really talk—I'd just asked Rebecca if . . . Oh, have you met?"

Rebecca smiles wanly. "No, you go upstairs," she says damningly. "I'm sure we can talk some other time."

"Come on," Lolli demands, pulling on my arm. "The night's still young."

And I'm being pulled away through the crowd, the others staring after me, Jerk with his mouth actually open, Tom shaking his head in disbelief.

"That was . . . ," I start to say angrily. But I'm supposed to be convincing Lolli to take me back to the convocation of vampires. So I shut up and climb the stairs between slumped, beer-stinky figures.

Bat is sitting at the top of the stairs, grinning a lazy grin and playing with a light-up yo-yo.

"Heya, sucker," says Lolli. "How's the thing?"

" 'T'sup, suckers," says Bat. "It's a good thing. Good time. Good party. I'm getting a little parched. Tell me when you're ready."

Lolli leads me by the hand down the hall, as if we were going to our bridal bed. The hall is low and badly lit and reeks of pot smoke. There's a line of girls outside the bathroom. After we go past them, I can hear them saying, disgusted, "Wasn't that Christopher what's-his-name? From, like, the freshman class or something?"

Now, I think, is the time to be evil. Now is wicked-ness time. I must agree to worship the Dark god

Tch'muchgar, and Lolli must not suspect anything. Once again, I am struck—the cosmic damage I may have caused dropping the Arm into Tch'muchgar's world—for who knows what Chet has in mind. *Undo what you have done,* that is what I'm thinking. *Undo what you have done.*

Everything hangs on this.

We step into what must be Kathy's bedroom and Lolli shuts the door behind us.

Because Kathy has been away at college, her room still has all the artifacts of girlhood in it, and some of the artifacts of womanhood. Plush bears and birds and moose are piled in a big googly-eyed Peaceable Kingdom on the bed, and awkward drawings of horses are pinned to the walls. Some bras hang on the closet door handle. There's a lot of lavender around.

"I'm, like, so glad you are coming," says Lolli, hugging me quickly.

"Let's go," I say. "We don't have long until they start the spells out on the lake and in the White Hen Pantry."

"Chris, this is, like, so great! We were so worried you were gonna ditch!"

"Lolli, I wouldn't miss this for the world."

"Okay! Let's go!"

"Whenever you're ready."

"Outta here, boy!"

"Let us," I say with some conviction, "burn some rubber."

"First thing. Right, just one thing." She taps me

naggingly on the shoulder. "You got to make a kill, brute."

I back one step toward the door. I can't think. "We don't have time," I say.

"No, man. You want to be part of the game, you have to be blooded."

"Blooded?"

"The blood from your first kill. Like, smeared on your cheeks." She raises her hand, and caresses first one of my cheeks, then the other, looking, the whole time, into my eyes. I look helplessly at her tan neck and the seamless way it fans out into her chest and breasts beneath the straps of her tank top. "You have to drink," she says.

"Oh?"

"Chet said. He said we couldn't trust you 'til you made your first kill. Chow time."

"Chet?"

"Chet. You know, Chet. Like, Mr. bad-ass-cool agent of Hell."

I am aware that this confirms my worst suspicions.

"We have to kill someone now?"

"Ding ding, soup's on." She snaps her fingers and sways her slim hips.

"You and Bat will help me? And . . . what's-her-name you came with? Asheleighe?"

Lolli looks at me for a moment impatiently. She is trying to decide whether I am worth the effort. She explains, "No. No, we will not be, like, aided and abetted by Hors d'oeuvre Asheleighe. We have imported Hors d'oeuvre Asheleighe specially from Pepperell, Mass., to be your victimo supremo. I made friends with her like a week ago. We shipped her in so she won't be traced. Jenny Whatsit hardly knows us and won't think to look when we hit the road."

She waits for me to reply. I am looking at her, but fidgeting with the belt loops on my jeans. I hike them up, then down. Up, then down. Panic. Quickly through my head flit squabbles—*Better to kill one girl and save a world? Greatest good for the greatest number of people?*—but there's no way. Teeth in her neck. Snapping of tendons. No way I can kill. Have to think of some way around—I fiddle with my belt loops, look at Lolli, and say, "Ah . . ."

Lolli Chasuble is getting a little angry with me. "Hello, Chris? Your problem is? Are you in or what?"

I bite my upper lip with my lower teeth. My belt loops have not lost their interest. Up, then down. Up, then down.

"Christ, we don't have time for this." She runs her hand nervously through her hair with a crackle of dried mousse. "You're gonna have to kill sometime, dude-o'-mine. Might as well be right now, tonight."

"I don't know."

"Don't know? Don't *know*? Like, *way* to be the most an*noy*ing person on earth. Do you know the . . . Never mind! What do I have to say? Omigod! Live a little!

You gonna stand there playing with your belt loops?"

"Lolli, I'm just having—"

"Shut up. Okay, look. You're not like getting it *through* your thick *head* that people are killers, too— they kill to save themselves just like yours truly. Think of that? That's what they do. That's what we do. No difference between us. And you're not like getting it *through* your thick *head* that it isn't a goddamn choice for you. You're going to be dead in a few weeks if you don't suck some major gore and quick." She steps forward, her hand on my arm, and her chest grazes mine. Her face is so close. So hard. "So don't waste my time, Chris. Let us all in on the secret. You gonna come out of the coffin? What's it going to be?"

"There must be—"

"Stop arguing!"

"I am not going to kill anyone!" I yelp. "Anyone I know! Forget it!"

"What are you up to? You're buying time." She's menacing. "You have a plan, don't you?"

"I wasn't . . ."

"You lie like shit. What do you think you're doing? Damn, man, you are . . . !"

"I have a respect for human life and—"

"Yeah? Go, girl! They don't have any respect for yours!"

"So you think I should just give up and throw in my whole life just so—"

"I think you're up shit's creek, is what I think!"

"—so I can go and dine with the damned!"

She glares at me. Her lips pull back and reveal her fangs. "Not 'damned,'" she hisses. "Just trying to live." And with that she moves swiftly past me to the door. She opens it. "Bat!" she calls.

I am used to having things happen to me, instead of me doing things. Now I realize that it is high time for me to do something quickly. Something escape-like. I have screwed up. She's looking angry, murderous, leaning out the door, her arm spread across it to bar my way. I crouch and fling myself into the hall. Bat is thumping down the hall toward me, bellowing like a Viking. "*Let's PARTEEEEEE! PARTEEEEE! OWWOWOWOW!*"

Then he sees me.

"What's the—?" he asks.

She's pointing at me and shouting, "Dickless here isn't going to—"

But I'm running low, trying to pass him.

He jabs his arm in my side. I slam against the wall and fall into a squat, but even then, I'm jumping forward toward the stairs.

I have to get into a large crowd. They can't risk a large crowd. He grabs at my shoe, but I'm slithering down the stairs like a snake, on my belly. Beer pools stain the carpet. Girls are screaming and standing up as I fall past them.

". . . so goddamn *drunk!*" one sneers.

And I'm in the thick of the party at the bottom of the stairs, and Bat in his muddy Keds is clomping down toward me with the look of an animal in his face.

My brother has gotten out his video camera and is trying to capture the essence of the party for future generations and anthropologists; big Pete Gallagher is growling, "Let me borrow it! Just one sec! Let me borrow it!"

"Come back here, *weeeeee-zull*!" I hear Bat yell.

"Let me borrow it!" says big Pete Gallagher and he yanks at it.

"Stop!" says Paul. "You're gonna screw up the picture!"

"Let me borrow it!"

"Okay, already. Here. Careful," says Paul. "The button on the side—"

"This?"

"No, look. No, don't do that one! God! No, you've got to push . . ."

Bat is shoving his way through the crowd toward me. Pete swings the camera around the room, saying, "Smile, man! Say 'Cheese!'"

Two of Pete's friends flex their muscles and say, "Cheese! Cheese, Petey-boy!"

"Careful!" says Paul, tagging along at Pete's side. "That's, like, an expensive piece of—"

"I'm careful! Be cool! I'm being careful!" says Pete, and he roars to Nicki Brown, "Bark! Bark like a dog! Up close and personal!" and he sticks the lens in her face and she's so drunk she barks like a dog.

Bat is pointing at me and only me from across the crowd.

He mouths the word "Die."

"Hey, care-careful!" says Paul again.

And I'm working my way toward the door.

"And the lovely Miss Lolli!" says Pete. "There's the lovely Miss Lolli! New acquaintance and playgirl of the month! Time for an up close and personal!"

"Careful!" says Paul. "I paid for that thing!"

"Yeah, yeah."

Lolli's just entered the room and they're clearing a way for her, and she's covering her face with her hand and saying, "Don't take pictures of me with that thing! I said: Don't take my picture!"

Pete has it in her face and now Bat has one eye on me but he's working his way toward her instead, yelling, "She said she doesn't like her *goddamn picture taken*! That means," he says, grabbing Pete's shoulder, "she *doesn't like her goddamn picture taken*!"

"Pete, please," mewls Paul. "That's—"

"This is my assistant, Paul," Pete explains to Bat, zeroing in on Lolli's chest. "Paul likes doing films of slugs. We're making footage for science." Everyone is laughing at my brother.

Paul still is hovering around the camcorder and Bat suddenly grabs it from Pete and yells at the top of his lungs, "*I'M GONNA BEAT THE CRAP OUT OF YOU IF YOU KEEP TAKIN' PICTURES OF THAT GIRL!*"

I dart out of the room—Pete's friends screaming, "Who the hell are you?" and Lolli screeching, "Get that thing out of my face!" and Paul whining, "Please, just give me the camera!" and Pete and Bat, they're both hollering at the top of their lungs, hardly words, just sounds.

And I'm out through the den, where an unwatched television shows *Pretty Woman,* and I'm through the kitchen, tripping in the dark, and suddenly I see there's someone in there, against the sink—

And by the light of the moon through the window, I see Hors d'oeuvre Asheleighe, her shirt open, and Trunk McIntyre is feeding on her neck.

For a moment, I'm transfixed in horror. Then, "Run!" I scream hoarsely. "Run!"

Trunk and Asheleighe recoil in surprise; Trunk spins around. "Shit!" he exclaims. "You watching? You little shit!"

And as I slam open the kitchen door and push my way through the crowd in the dining room I can hear her saying, "God, that kid is, like, can you say schitzoid?"

And the dining room leads to the front door. I can hear them in the living room—

"I said get it out of my face and I meant get it out of my face!"

"What's the problem? You jealous?"

"Hey, please give me my—"

"Damn!"

"*Watch—!*"

And I'm out the front door and into the night.


It's after ten, and I've blown it. I've blown my cover. I don't know how I'll find the conclave of vampires now, or how I would get there if I found it. The conclave is miles away. The town's spells of binding will be interrupted in less than two hours.

I am wandering around the fairground, full of the knowledge that I have endangered the world, and my body is sliding into a murderous thirst, and I can do nothing to stop either thing.

And worse than that, I am being sought. They want my blood, one way or another. I turn around often as I skulk from tent to tent, and I make sure that Bat and Lolli aren't slinking up behind me through the ranks of half-shirts and flip-flops.

On the loudspeaker, we are coming to the goat part of the evening. The mayor is talking about it. "Let's prepare the elements. Can, uh, can everyone at the other sites hear me?"

"Yes, Ed."

"Sure, Ed. We're reading you loud and clear."

"Thanks. First we'll, uh, prepare the goats. Out on the boat, we have Sal Garozzi, butcher at the Purity

Supreme in Bradley. Sal has kindly offered, once again, to do the honors. You there, Sal?"

"I am, Ed."

"How's it looking, Sal?"

Sal considers for a minute. "Well, it's looking pretty nice out tonight. There's a moon. Oh, you mean the lake? The lake is calm."

I can't see the lake from here because of the trees, but I can see the three radio towers, their lights winking regularly like breaths softly hissed into the night.

That is when I spy Rebecca. She is walking with Tom and Kristen toward the tilt-a-whirl. Jerk bobs along behind them. I can see Rebecca laugh deep and long.

Above them all, there is the monotonous sound of the butcher, the mayor, and the town selectmen sacrificing a goat to cosmic forces. They say, "We cry out to you that the Dark may be bound. We cry out to you, O, shining sentinels, for strength in the night.

"And now we shall bind the foe, by your grace. And now with the blood of this living creature, and with these malleable spirits, we follow the silver cord into Darkness," the voice calls out.

I feel lighter just looking at her. Rebecca, who told me she would talk to me. Rebecca, who knows spells.

Suddenly, the screaming of the goat starts.

"Get the goat. Get that damn goat!" someone out on the lake yells over the loudspeaker.

It screams again.

People stop what they're doing—stop licking their ice creams, passing their tokens, playing their games. They look up.

There's a silence. Kristen has covered her ears.

There's a trickling noise over everything. It is brief and poignant.

I run toward Rebecca and the rest, all of them together, while above us, strung on wires and poles, the incantations continue, booming: "Hear us, O Tch'muchgar, Melancholy One, Vampire Lord. Hear us and despair. You shall be blinded with light. You shall be bound in radiance. You shall stare, unblinking, at the light that sears you, and burns you, and claims you, for all eternity."

Rebecca's step is light; and her sandaled feet arch on the grass as they did long ago, bare, that night when I saw her with her sister at Persible Dairy.

I want to embrace her.

Suddenly, as if cued by Rebecca's beauty, the air is filled with the cooing of distant police sirens, like pretty birds rising all around from a Persian palace court.

And I am by her side.


"Rebecca," I call. "Rebecca!"

"Hey, Chris," they all say as I run up.

"What happened to that girl?" says Chuck. "Lolli whatever?"

"I don't know," I say, trying to sound nonchalant

but looking wildly over my shoulder, past the Dizzy Caterpillar. "She's trying to find me. There's safety in numbers."

"Especially ten, in the Cabala," Rebecca offers idly, looking sideways. "That's the number of the Sephiroth." Everyone finds that a bit of a conversation stopper. For a minute, we all think of what to say next.

Then Andy says, "Hey, want to go on the tilt-a-whirl?"

Everyone says yeah and starts to head over to it, Tom and Andy and Chuck looking back at me and whispering among themselves. They are whispering: Why is he running away from Lolli? Boy, if she were looking for me, man, I sure wouldn't be hiding, it would be ollie, ollie in-come-free. Jerk trudges beside them, looking guilty and upset at hearing bad things about me. Kristen walks up between Tom and Chuck.

"Rebecca," I say. "I—" For the moment, that seems enough. Then I continue, "Rebecca, I need to talk to you."

She stops. She hesitates, poised as if standing on top of a column. "What's wrong?" she asks and follows the lines of my face with her eyes. "You look really sick." She turns all the way toward me.

I shrug. "I need to talk to you," I say helplessly. "Could we talk?"

"Of course. I told you . . ." She nods. "You could come with me on the tilt-a-whirl."

I look ahead at the tilt-a-whirl. It flings people around at fifty miles per hour, their hair streaming, their mouths open, their hands clutching at the sides of the car. I admit, "I'm not sure we'd reach any definite conclusions after talking on the tilt-a-whirl."

Rebecca nods. "Just a sec," she says in shorthand. She jogs up to Kristen and whispers something in her ear.

Kristen points at me and says something to Chuck, Tom, and Andy. The three of them start laughing and glancing back at me.

I don't care. I glance up at their necks, craned back to look at me, and at the wiry tendons there, and I think a passing thought about how pleasant it would be to kill them and feel their blood moving through me.

But now Rebecca is at my side, smiling uneasily.

"Come on," I say to her hoarsely. "Come on."

"What is it?" she demands. "What?"

"Come on!"

"No. Tell me."

"Please," I say.

And I think my eyes are so desperate, as are the corners of my mouth and other regions of my face, that she silently follows me.

We run through the crowds.

People are wolfing down fried dough. People are prowling in packs. A child is screaming by the moonwalk, "My arm is broke! My arm is broke!" People are shoving and grabbing.

Lights spin over us. There's screaming all around. And above it all, voices booming out over the gruesome disco from the merry-go-round, "We damn him in his thought. We damn him in his speech. We damn him in his being. Our hate is ranged against him."

The crowds push; people sing; someone barfs behind a tent. His back heaves again and again, as if it's being wrung.

"A hot dog! A hot dog! I wanna hot dog!" yowls a child dragging a bear by the ear, but her parents are lost in the crowd.

And I lead Rebecca through it all to a grove of trees off to the side.

And we stand there, together, in the warm summer's night.

The moon is pale above the whirling lights and is fringed by silver wings of cloud. The trees rustle softly above us, as if anxious with sap.

The smell of the grass is sweet, and the night feels wide and the adventure good; and I feel we can, together, do something. We will pound on desks; we will point at the map and direct the police and use words like "zone six," "ETA," and "triangulation."

Finally.

"Chris," she says, stepping toward me. "You are so strange sometimes." She says it gently, so gently it's like she's stroking my face. (She isn't.) She leans back against a tree trunk, her legs stiff. Her toe is touching mine. I don't know if she notices. I wriggle my toe closer to her toe. Softly, she urges me, "I'm ready for your revelation. Whatever it is."

Finally. Finally.

"Rebecca," I say (I can't believe I'm saying the name!), "it is very hard to talk about."

She nods her head. "I can see. Don't worry."

"I have to explain something."

She laughs lightly. "Yes, you do."

"But I will explain myself."

She pushes herself up with her hands outspread, so she is standing close to me. "You have to be brave," she says.

She is standing very close to me. Her arms are at her sides, but they don't need to be. If they moved up any, they would be around me. My arms would be around her. She is looking up into my face and searching it; her lips are parted.

Her neck is turned to look up at me, and I can almost feel its silky grass-sweet skin, follow its curve down past her collarbone and the fluting of her throat to her soft chest. My teeth are moving. They are becoming fangs. I need to talk quickly.

"Rebecca, there's something . . . You'll have to trust me."

Her skin is beautifully cool and white in the moonlight, as cool and white as a tomb. And beneath it, her blood races. "Look, Chris, you've got to stop beating around the bush." She puts her hand on my arm and rubs it up and down to reassure me. It does not reassure me. My teeth are swelling because of the blood. They're enormous. They're crowding the rest of my mouth. I can barely move my tongue.

It is now. Now or never.

I reach up and almost take her hand. Leaning toward her, I murmur urgently, "Rebecca, you have to underththand—under—"

"What?" She leans toward me, holding my arm.

My teeth are huge. "I thaid, you—I *thaid*—"

"What?"

"I, uh, it'th jutht—it'th—ohhhhhhhhhh, thit!" I wail. I turn from her and smack a tree ineffectually. "Thit! Thit! Thit! Thit! Thit!" I hide my mouth with my hand.

My teeth are mammoth; tusklike; throbbing; barely crammed into my mouth.

I am filled with rage. I don't even know at what. Rebecca looks at me, maybe even frightened. I stagger back away from her like a cowering animal. "Chris?" she says.

I am ready to pounce. Her neck is spread out, her arms, her chest—I want to feed on her. I want to kill her. I back away. I run back toward the fairground, screaming petulantly, "No! No! No! Oh, thit, thit, thit, thit, *thit*!"

Back through the crowds of screaming teens, back through the teeming maze of stalls.

"Chris!" she calls.

But I am all alone; I know that now. I am all alone with the Forces of Darkness ranged against me.

I lope down the littered aisles, wild with longings.

Lolli—I am thirsty; and she is evil. Kill two birds with one stone. That is my plan: Kill two birds with one stone. Drink Lolli's blood. I will drink Lolli's blood to stay alive.

As I run on, the thoroughfares are empty, the fairground air dank with chill. Something has happened. Now no one smiles in the sweet-smelling stable decay of the tents and tarps; a few fat faces gawk as I stumble past stalls; and they turn and talk.

I notice now that grandparents grimly grab their sticky charges as I hurtle past and on and on, past the narrowed eyes of lone fair-folk, leaning against their machines—the ferris wheel deserted, the teacups drained to the dregs—past a gaggle of girls, their limbs ripe and red; past a cluster of couples holding babies (sacks of blood as succulent as grapes)—I am thirsty; she is evil—kill two birds with one stone—I tear through the fair, gasping for breath, greedy for gore, I sprint across the lawn to the Rigozzis', stumble up the steps, almost crowing for the kill . . .

And silence greets me.

The house blares with light, but there is no sound. There is no sound but the agitation of crickets that have seen things.

The door is ajar.

I slip in.

The music is off. Overturned beer cups drool on the carpeted stairs.

Something is wrong.

I step gingerly into the living room. The stereo is on, but the CD player mute. No one is there to listen. Paul's camcorder lies crumpled and kicked on the floor. Chairs are overturned; the table where Lolli danced and bucked is broken; and I look up and see, splattered across the wall, the stains where a head with blood-wet hair slammed down and slid.

Carefully, I approach the blotch. It is already beginning to dry.

The beer keg drips in the silence.

*Plick. Plick. Plick. Plick.*

I examine the first impact where the head must have hit, the trail where it smeared down to the baseboard.

*Plick. Plick. Plick.*

The sprinkled droplets are drying to black.

*Plick. Plick.*

"This is not a good party."

I whip around; I stagger backward. The voice is coming from the other side of a sofa turned away from me. Carefully, I approach. Some sophomore stoner sits there, staring vacantly away from me. I can tell at a glance that he is baked. He looks tiny slumped on the sofa, lost in a pool of his own huge clothes.

"Who is that there?" he asks. "Knock-knock. Knock-knock!"

"No one," I whisper. "No one thpecial."

I back away to the wall.

I draw my lips together. I crouch down so I'm below his line of sight. I'm hunkered next to the wall, ready to sprint.

"Man," he says. "Ma-ha-ha-ha-han." He sighs. "Ma-ha-ha-ha-han."

"What happened?" I ask, almost in a whisper.

For a minute, he just sits there, still staring in the opposite direction. I can no longer see him over the back of the sofa. "This . . . She didn't show up on film. She. Pete Gallagher. He. You know Pete?"

I want to get him talking. "I know Pete," I say. "What happened?"

Carefully, watching the back of the sofa, I lean and put my cheek against the wall. I stick my tongue out and begin licking the blood.

"Man, ma-ha-ha-ha-han." I hear him shift slightly. "He was taking this video, you know. There was this, and it, this guy with her. He started to. You know. Beat out of, I mean, the crap out of Pete. The crap."

I'm crazed and nervous in the quiet, just listening to the monotone of his idiot voice over the distant crickets through the open door. I press my cheek closer to the wall and keep lapping silently at the salty scum.

"They started to punch at first. Then it turned into

this whole big fight. This whole big fight. Chaos. Complete chaos." His voice is sliding up the scale, getting higher and whinier. "He killed Pete, I think. I think Pete is dead. God. I think he's . . . bought the farm. A hundred and twenty acres of the best, man. Cattle and pastures. With a ding-dong here, and a ding-dong there."

My tongue rasps against the drying clots. I realize he's stopped talking. Got to get him going again. I open my eyes, panting, draw my tongue in, and ask, "Tho what happened then?" Go back to licking.

"Then that bitch. What's her name? She ran and tried to get away. She and this guy, running down the driveway. People thought they were just going to get away?"

Faintly, from upstairs, I hear careful footsteps.

They start in Kathy's bedroom.

"Tony, he . . . There. He got in his car, drove full speed into her. Bam! She couldn't be killed but I guess that did . . ." He sighs again, and shifts slightly. "The trick. She went flying, man. Flew. Broke her back. She was out. Knocked out. They called the police. Took her into town for a . . . you know. Execution. Formally."

The footsteps stalk down the carpeted hallway toward the stairs. I don't know who it is, but it sounds as if whoever is making the footsteps is walking softly, so as not to be heard.

"If I ever see that bitch again," the stoner drones, "man, I'm not going to give her the time. Not the Time. Of. Day. No way."

I really want to run, but the blood is too good, even in dried flakes like fish food. I rise. I bob down to get a quick last lick at the scab, then briskly make my way toward the front door. The footsteps upstairs pick up.

"Can't. How can she do that to Pete, man? Just do that. To, like, the captain of lacrosse."

The footsteps are racing down the steps from upstairs. I hurtle out through the door.

Down the steps. I pound down the driveway toward the main road.

Looking back, I see a shape throwing itself down the front stairs. Someone is running after me, arms flailing with speed.

I'm almost down the driveway, darting through little pools of light from lamps among the rhododendrons.

My feet slap the tarmac. I'm hurtling down the slope toward the road.

I am on the main road. I turn left, the direction of the fair.

The streetlights along the narrow road cast a ghastly sheen over the cracks and rubble where the road fades to forest.

Gasping for breath, I pound toward the field where people are parked.

I have to reach a crowd. I have to reach a crowd.

I have to tell them not to kill her.

I can hear footsteps clattering down the driveway.

They have to stop the killing. For one thing, she

knows where to find the convocation of vampires. So I have to stop them.

My shirt is untucked, my mouth hanging open, dragging at the air.

My tongue, in spite of everything, still stings and squirms in happy memory.

I hurtle toward the fair.

I jump roadkill.

I look back.

Bat, sprinting toward me. Suddenly slowing and stopping. Looking past me.

I turn; look.

Right behind me, Chet flickers and solidifies. His teeth glint like iron in the dim light.

He grabs my wrists and yanks them up above my head.

He shakes his head like he is disappointed, and chides, "Christopher, you've got to stop running."

And from behind, I hear the doom-filled tread of Bat's Keds on the tarmac.

**CHAPTER 8** Chet stands before me, the whites of his eyes faintly glowing with a sick pearly light. "Almost midnight," he says. "Almost time for all Hell to break loose." He yanks my arms again, and I twitch in pain.

"Who *are* you?" I hiss.

"My name is not important, Christopher. We're going to see your handiwork now. The fruit of your labor. Couldn't have done it without you." He's clearly enjoying himself.

Bat steps out of the shadows, his stubbly face weird with snarls. He points at me, yells, "BASTARRRD! He's mine. *Miiiiiine!* Give me the bastard. Give him to me, Chet."

"No, Bat," says Chet. "I can't do that."

"*Give him to meeeee!*" Bat screams. "*MEEEEEE!*" He swings his fists. "He's the reason they've got her! *GIVE HIM TO MEEEEE!*"

Chet drops my arms.

"They don't have her anymore, Bat," he says lazily. "I'm afraid your succulent, truculent friend was executed just three and a half minutes ago. You can see the footage on the news. They took her to the town center." His voice harsh with pleasure, he continues, "I understand her body started to knit back together on the ride over. By the time they got her into town, she was awake. She started struggling. The police went to take her out of the car and transport her into the courthouse. Unfortunately, she lashed out. One of the officers tripped and fell. The crowd couldn't be controlled. It was a mob scene. They found sharp things. Someone must have found a stake. They killed her where she fell, with her head and half her back on the pavement and the lower half of her body trailing in the gutter. She didn't even die on level ground. Somehow that hurts particularly, don't you think?"

Bat looks lost. He's pale. Pale as a ghost.

"Sorry, Bat. She's not here anymore. She's gone. Damned."

Bat is limp. "I've got to talk to her," he whimpers. "But I've got to talk to her."

Chet shrugs. "Okay," he says. Suddenly, his voice is high—his voice is hers—and he screams, "Help me, Bat! Help me! I'm in so much *pain*!!!" He smiles blandly, and says, "It goes on like that for a while. All eternity."

"You *bastard*! *YOU BASTARD!*" yells Bat, moving toward Chet. He slaps his hand down to his belt and pulls out an ornate and ancient switchblade, rune covered and flashing with little sparks of fire.

Bat yowls and throws himself at Chet, raising the wild dagger.

He flies across the clearing.

Chet waves his hand, and Bat disappears.

The woods are in turmoil. The trees still warp and shudder in the wind, and the leaves still spin as if propelled.

"Where did he go?" I ask, breathless.

Chet looks up and down the empty road, obviously pleased with himself. "He was no longer useful," he says. He claps once. "Now I want to see what you've made possible, Christopher. They'll be sacrificing the final goat soon. So step lively. Move." He grabs my shoulders, turns me, pushes me toward the woods. I stumble between the trees.

Chet lifts his legs above fallen branches; he holds back the spiny limbs of saplings for me to pass. The road gets smaller behind us. We're headed down the slope toward the bank of the reservoir.

"What's going on?" I demand.

"On?" says Chet.

I shove through a stand of pine that writhes with our passage. "Tell me what's going on," I say.

"Isn't it a little late for that question?" Chet asks. "Maybe you should have thought of that earlier."

"I did," I say sourly. "I was tricked."

"I'm so sorry," he says. "I'm very sorry to hear that you were tricked."

The night is uneasy and electrical as we pace along through the forest at a furious clip. The clouds are low and discolored; but the moon still shines. Through the trees, the lake burns an electric blue. Strange currents slip along power lines and rock the trees and prod the crickets to chirp like clockwork mechanisms.

Through the loose branches of pine, I can see the reservoir. Out in the center, the light bobs from the sacrificial boat. Beyond it, little isles rise, then the blinking radio towers and the dark hills beneath the moon.

"Pick it up. There's not a moment to spare," Chet says.

We run silently through the woods. I have to run to keep up with him. His strides have gained in urgency. He bangs boughs out of his way with unfeeling arms. Tramples through brambles. Scampers over boulders. And I run to follow him.

He holds out his hand and guides me down a wall of rock.

We stand on the banks of the Wompanoag Reservoir. The clouds are dense and draining across the sky. The crickets sing as if in fever.

"Here, so you can follow the action, let me galvanize something. You'll be able to hear our vampiric counterstrike," says Chet, taking a nickel out of his pocket. He rubs it twice with his thumb, and it starts to speak.

It blares: ". . . give us the cue, we'll continue with the ritual as scheduled. We must not panic."

And: "No, certainly not, Mayor. We're ready to continue here."

"A-OK, Father Bread?"

"Lay your hand upon this wilderness that the wicked and untoward may not stalk within it. Smother us with peace, O guardians of Light."

"Soon," mutters Chet. "Soon."

"Bless us in this time of trial. Place your seal upon the waters of Wompanoag and the valley where once our ancestors roamed. Place the ancient seal of holding upon those hills and forests, that Darkness may not—"

And then there is a burst of static.

Nonsense voices keening and screaming.

The squealing of wind instruments untuned and blown without rhyme or reason.

People screaming in Latin; screaming in Greek; screaming profanity.

". . . seem to have some static on your line . . ."

And ripples start to shoot across the lake.

Vampire voices scream blasphemy and blood.

Chet is licking his lips. His eyes fly from one point to the other, absorbed.

"The spell of interruption," he says. "I'd give it one more minute." Slowly, statically, like a statue unfolding, he lays his arms out straight on either side. And as he does so, there is a low hum of power. I hear him whispering beneath his breath, "Lord, make me an instrument of your discord." His fingers begin to twitch with blue fire. On either hand, his slim fingers wheel like the branches that thrash around us.

"No!" I scream as the wind starts to howl. "No!"

And I throw myself at Chet, and pass through his body, and slam to the ground on the other side of him.

His head is back, his mouth thrown open, his eyes rolling uncontrollably. His skull rocks as if his neck is broken. A bulb of blue flame smokes on each outspread hand. His body pops and flares, sections blurring and fading and snapping back into focus.

The lake is in turmoil. The waters boil and rock.

Lines of light have started to burn from point to point, stretching to the unseen sites where, in the town forest and the White Hen Pantry, the people chant old rites.

On the water flickers a triangle of red.

Chet flashes; is there; is not; is.

His body is burning with blue fire.

"Kneel!" he roars. "Kneel before the power of the Melancholy One! Tch'muchgar, Vampire Lord, we welcome you!"

The nickel lies on the ground, searing the leaves, howling with voices, with cries, with screams of fear. Blasts of static crack through the night.

Chet screams weird words—his throat pops and spatters with power—

And in the midst of the triangle, thrashing above the lake, I see the Vampire Lord.

A dim maw—vast—outlined—the huge motion of something so massive that the mountains ripple— howling.

With a cry that courses through the heavens—knocks stars spinning—wallops leagues of hills—the Dark Lord leaps.

And there is a burst of energy.

A crack of thunder.

The sky turns to day.

The lake smashes with fire.

I scream.

And then he is gone.


My eyes are fixed for a while on the ground. Princess pines cluster around the base of a tree. The crickets have gone silent. The wind has dropped, exhausted to nothing. When I look up, Chet is sitting on the ground, resting his elbows on his knees, looking out at the lake. The lake is quiet; dead. Fish bob belly-up in the reeds.

"Where is he?" I ask.

"Gone," says Chet softly.

I wait. I look suspiciously out at the shapeless hills and the inane blinking of the radio towers. Out in the middle of the lake, the town selectmen splash near their overturned boat. Their tiny mewling voices drift over the water. "Where is—" "Help! Help!" "Is that *thing* in here? *Is it in here?* Get me—I thought I saw—" The water tinkles as they scrabble with the boat, way out in the vast center of the reservoir.

Finally I say, "Gone where?"

"Nowhere. Dead. Tch'muchgar doesn't exist. The Arm of Moriator destroyed him. Remember, you placed it there yourself, Christopher." Chet softly taps his knees with his fingers. "When Tch'muchgar tried to escape, the Arm kicked in. It displaced his prison world; he leaped out and slipped into the crack between worlds. He no longer exists. Gone."

Slowly, I look straight at Chet's face. There is a look of serene triumph, a kind of hidden sweet glee there. All the sarcasm and cruelty has gone out of him. I feel a kind of shuddering hope move throughout my body, starting with my chest.

Chet is still tapping on his knees. What he's tapping sounds like "I've got rhythm, I've got music, I've got my girl, who could ask for anything more?"

I can't believe it. I'm almost laughing. "He's really gone?" I insist.

"Yes, he really is. Forever." Chet smiles at me. "Congratulations to both of us."

I laugh. It is a ragged little laugh, a little hoarse cough-y thing that would not get much on the open market—but it is a laugh nonetheless. A human laugh. "I, um. You know? I thought you were working for the vampires."

"No," says Chet. "I had the appearance of that, but I would never work for vampires. Not seriously. I needed them to interrupt the spells of warding so that Tch'muchgar would be freed up for just one crucial moment. Just long enough for him to jump and be destroyed. I guess I'm a double agent. Christopher, I might even be a triple agent."

He rises, clapping his hands together to shake out the kinks in his muscles.

"So, you were just using the vampires? I mean, Bat and everyone?"

"Mmmm, yes. Poor, poor Bat. For a strapping thing of a hundred and seventy-two, that boy certainly doesn't act his age."

I do my ragged laugh again. Then I say, "Do you know how relieved I am?"

"No, Christopher. How relieved are you?"

"I am more relieved than a very relieved thing from Planet Phew."

He nods. "I'm happy to hear you're that relieved," he says. "It does my old heart good."

"I thought you were a servant of the Forces of Darkness," I explain.

"You didn't!" replies Chet.

"I did."

"Well, I'm not," says Chet, shaking his head.

"See, and that's why I'm relieved."

"Well might you be relieved," he agrees. "And you can lay your fears to rest. I have never been and never will be a servant of the Forces of Darkness. I'm a mercenary, of course. I work for them freelance, on a job-by-job basis."

At this, my head shoots up. He's not facing me. His grin has changed a little bit. Now I can see his teeth. They are gray.

A few lone crickets start wheezing hoarsely.

"What?" I say.

"I said I work for them freelance. On a job-by-job basis."

I scramble to get to my feet. He's looking proudly out across the lake, as if he has just finished gluing all the trees and islands there. The crickets are picking up, more and more of them chittering.

"What do you mean?"

"I think I've just explained this. I work for the Forces of Darkness, Christopher, but on a freelance basis. Meaning, I'm employed by Tch'muchgar."

"Tch'muchgar? But you just killed him. Do you mean, Tch'muchgar—the Vampire Lord?"

"Christopher, it's not a common name."

"I don't understand."

Chet turns and finally looks at me. "Would you like me to explain?" he asks me.

The crickets are calling to one another in gasping choirs.

"I think it would be obvious to you by now, Christopher. Locked up like that with nothing to think about, nothing to do but hate his captors, hate himself for his failure, hate life—the only escape he wanted in the end was escape from his own tedious, circular, dream-starved thoughts. There's nothing Tch'muchgar wanted to do more than die. But of course, he couldn't. Completely powerless. That was the hell of it. Couldn't even move, figuratively speaking, to slit his own wrists." Chet stops for a moment. Broods on his tale. Rubs his hand over his face. "God he was depressing." He sighs.

"Enter: me. I was drifting without direction, disembodied, between worlds, looking for work, when, lo, I heard a voice from on high, saying to me, 'Blessed are the dead, for they rest from their labors.' It was Tch'muchgar—completely suicidal, unable to move, only barely able to cry out.

"An agreement was made; we settled on a price. I reentered your time-stream about twenty years ago and began to make arrangements. I prodded the vampires into action, promised them a Golden Age, another reign of the Vampire Lord. About a year ago, I made a sweep through the area, disembodied, and settled on you as the most likely of several local vampire cubs. You were obviously going to ripen at just the right time. I needed someone who could slip past the vampires, but who would be willing to activate the Arm of Moriator by invoking Light. A vampire would have suspected something. But you? It was all a masterstroke on my part, Christopher. I'm sorry to gloat; it's just that I'm rather wonderful."

The crickets' crazed fluting shimmers around us like music for a wild, nervous dance. The goat dark woods are full of it. I'm wary; frightened; we are alone on the bank, and the forest is wide. He's still smiling at me like an uncle with a five-dollar bill hidden in one of his hands.

"What have you done to me?" I say. "What have you done?"

"Nothing. You were doomed before I saw you." He folds his hands primly in front of him.

"No, you've got to tell me. What about me now?" I try to sound strong. I'm hysterical. He can hear I'm afraid. He can hear I'm almost whimpering.

"What? Now?"

"My vampirism."

"I'm so sorry."

"You lied about that. You lied about being able to help me."

He laughs kindly. "Of *course* I lied, Christopher," he says. "What did I just say I am? I'm a freelance agent of the Forces of Darkness. I'm *supposed* to lie. I lie, cheat, kill, make people unhappy, and draw an enormous wage."

"I helped you! I did everything you asked!"

"Christopher, Christopher, Christopher! It's not within my power! I can't change what you are. You are what you are. I could remold the matter you're made of to make you human, like a wizard turning a shepherdess into a frog, but you wouldn't be yourself. Everything about you is vampiric. Your jaws are vampire jaws. Your teeth are retractable vampire teeth. Your heart is a vampire heart with little wicked tendrils strapped around your ribs, strangling your other organs. Your mind—cold, distant, hungry—everything—you're a vampire, Christopher. An honest-to-gosh bloodsucking son of the damned."

"What can I do?" I demand, snapping my arms out straight. "What?"

Chet shrugs. "Not much. You're going to die soon, Christopher. Unnatural causes, one way or another. Try to enjoy what little time you have left. You could go on a killing spree, draw the blood you need, but without guidance you'll soon get caught and lynched. It's a shame your little friend Lolli didn't survive," he says with a leer. "That girl was sufficiently acrobatic to liven up the final months of any young man worth his salt."

"I'll turn myself in," I threaten him. "I'll tell them what's happened."

Chet shakes his head. "Is that wise, Christopher? Is that really wise? Don't forget that you're guilty of first-degree deicide. Killing a god. The Forces of Light will demand to try you. Tch'muchgar was their prisoner. They wanted him to live. They'll find you guilty and commence torture. Believe me, they'll take advantage of the fact that you can't die of normal causes. Do you really want to spend all of eternity that way, Christopher? Being tortured slowly by white faceless glowing beings?"

"Of course, you won't be much better off at home.

You're going to go insane soon. You're going to kill someone. If for some reason you don't, you're going to fall into a coma, starved. Either way, you're bound to have a stake driven through your heart. This is a diverting little problem, isn't it, Christopher?"

I wait for him to go on. His face brightens and he says, "Here, let's think about this idea."

"What?" I grunt.

"You could go join the vampire band. They'd teach you the rudiments of killing and concealment. Offer emotional support. That might be the only place you'd be safe . . ."

"You think I should?"

"But, of course, you have unfortunately just murdered their god and sole hope of victory. Soon they'll figure it out; then they'll bite your throat out. So I guess that isn't such a good idea after all." He shrugs. "You know what, Christopher? You're screwed. Well, I'm going now."

"You bastard," I say, stunned. "You are a complete bastard."

"Not so far off the truth," he agrees blandly. "Hypostatic parthenogenesis."

"You can't just leave me."

"Of course I can. I'll take a lot of pleasure in it, too."

"You can't leave!"

"Not without slapping you first," he agrees and slaps me for no reason.

I stagger back against a tree.

"It takes so little," he muses, "to cause biological beings pain." His leg swipes upward and catapults into my shin. I topple on the ground, swearing and clutching. "Very strange." He titters. "I've been given so much power, Christopher, so much in payment for this little gig. I feel almost young again. Do you understand? I'm seeing new things! I'll be like a god soon! Despoiling worlds! A reign of terror! Ha!" He performs a quick dance upon the summer moss.

I'm rising to my feet as he hops in his jig. I'm careful, slow, ready to attack.

Above him, the horrified moon looks down through the black branches of pine. He trots and skips, chuckling and hopping, clapping and laughing beneath the night sky.

My teeth are now moving, they're sliding and pointing, they're ready for battle and blood in my veins.

He's tapping and spinning and whirling and laughing; he's hooting great names in the still of the night.

I take a step forward.

I scowl.

And I pounce.

*Whack!* His fist flies out, and I go careening backward, my nose splattering blood down my face.

I'm on all fours again, kneeling in the moss.

Blood in my mouth.

I'm thirsty now. I lick at it quickly.

His shoes move across the moss toward me.

I'm hungry for the attack. I tense my muscles.

"It's bad manners to kick a man when he's down," Chet says, "but it's just Too! Much! Damn! Fun!" and with each word, he delivers a savage kick in my side or my arm or my head.

I roll.

I can't tell which way is up. I feel the weight of my body, but can't tell how it's falling. My lips are sticky. Sticky. I lick them. I want his blood.

"Why me?" I gasp. I want his blood.

"Why did I choose you, Christopher? Because you threw the Forces of Light off my trail," he says. "They thought that because you were a child, you were innocent, working for them. It took them months to figure out the truth. And by the time they did, you were marked as mine; there was nothing they could do." His voice is ringing in my head—all around me, like a halo of feedback in burning red. "But do you know the other reason I chose you, Christopher? Because I knew you were an incompetent: self-pitying; self-absorbed; self-centered. The perfect teen. I knew you wouldn't ask the right questions at the right time. In other words," he says, leaning down and placing his hand kindly on my crippled shoulder, "I chose you because, to quote Tom, your best friend in this world, you are a complete peckerhead."

He stands upright.

I lunge for his feet.

I pass through them, and he stands with his foot on my head.

He rocks the heel against my forehead. "No, Christopher. You won't win this one."

I am thinking wildly in my head, under his foot. What I realize is he must take me with him. I must become his assistant. I will help him in his evil; then one day, I will turn. I will betray him.

"You've got to take me with you. I'll help you."

"Good-bye, Christopher."

"You've got to! You made me what I am!"

"No, I didn't. Good-bye."

"Chet! Pleathe! I can help you. We can work together."

"No, we can't, Christopher. I can read your thoughts now, and they're stupid."

"Chet!"

"That's not my name. You don't even know my name."

The foot lifts off me.

I lunge again.

Again I fall through him.

He steps back.

"You can't—"

"I can."

"No, Chet!"

"That's not my name."

"Pleathe!"

"No."

"God, pleathe!"

"Good-bye."

"I'm tho alone! *I'm tho alone!*" I scream, terrified.

For a moment, the un-celestial being eyes me up and down. Almost with compassion. Then slowly, whimsically, he recites, "In the midst of life, we are in death. Of whom may we seek for succor, sucker?"

He smiles at me.

Then he vanishes and leaves me appalled; for I know, and realize, that all he has said is true.

# EPILOGUE

I am in my room.

I'm grounded for staying out after midnight. Somehow, that does not seem important to me now.

I look at my posters on my wall and at the stack of CDs next to my CD player. They don't seem like mine anymore. I don't want to listen to any of them. I don't want to look at the posters. They are of someone else's favorite thrash bands. They are covered with someone else's clever comments in black and silver magic markers. So I tear them down and crumple them up.

For a minute, I consider drawing big Xs on the walls where they hung. But I can't. It would take too long. Instead, I throw the pen against the wall. I pick it up and throw it again. I can't be violent enough to the pen, so I twist it and step on it until it breaks and spreads ink on the tasteful wall-to-wall carpeting.

Earlier today, I saw Lolli die on TV. We were all sitting around the television, eating together and watching the news, like everyone else in town. They were showing the footage as I came back from throwing up.

Even with the special lens filters they use, Lolli hardly showed up on the screen.

". . . Unfortunately, the police did not manage to get the vampiress inside the courthouse. During the ride from the Rigozzi house, where she was first injured, she regained consciousness. It appears that the substantial contusions, breaks, and fractures she sustained as a result of the automobile impact had healed to such an extent that when the police attempted to remove her from the vehicle, she attacked. Fortunately, her spine was still snapped, leaving her unable to move the lower half of her body. The crowd . . ."

I didn't listen any longer. The words were a babble. I just watched.

It had all happened as Chet said it had. The police went to take Lolli out of the car and transport her into the courthouse. She lashed out. One of the escorts tripped and fell. The crowd couldn't be controlled. They swarmed in around her. She tried to fight them or run, her eyes rolling crazily, her hips lying motionless in the muck of the gutter.

People poured around her with knives, with stones, with bits of glass. Each one taking their turn to gouge. Piling on top of one another. Screaming and yelling. Then I couldn't see her. People were all around her. They were on top of her. She was gone beneath them. She was gone.

At the back of the crowd, I saw Chet. He was there before the courthouse, standing at the back of the crowd, his face red and distorted with rage, shaking his fist, urging them on to kill her.

". . . of sixteen apparent years of age. Her companion, nicknamed Bat, is still at large. Peter Gallagher, the teen injured in the first heroic struggle with the vampires, was rushed to the hospital, where he is reported to be in serious condition."

They interviewed Mayor Pensonville. He straightened his tie pin. "It was a brave thing Peter Gallagher and Anthony Rigozzi did. I'd like to shake those young men's hands. It took something to stand up to these vampires. If everyone in this country had that something, then maybe, just maybe, there would be less vampires, and more—" (he hesitated) "more streets that would be safe for our children. All I can say is 'Bravo! to them' and 'Vampires beware!'" He held up a finger. "I pledge— yes, I pledge: We will not stop until our children are safe to walk on the streets at night! We all are on the lookout!"

I turn and see that my mother has put down her fork and is watching me. Her eyes blink quickly, nervously. "Tomorrow we're going down to see the doctor again. We're going down there tomorrow, and if it turns out that all this time—if it turns out you're a vam—" She can't say the word. Her face twists around it, looking frightened and dangerous, and it won't come out.

"Goddamn, Mom," says my brother, glaring at her. He slams back his chair and leaves the table.

She points. "I'm telling you. If you're—"

Again, she just shakes her head.

My father looks at his empty plate.

*No,* I think to myself as I throw up again in the bathroom. *She would not turn me in. My own mother would not. She would not actually turn me in.*

Sometime in the afternoon, Jerk calls.

*Brrring brrring. Brrring brrring.*

"Christopher," says my father through the door. "It's for you. It's Je—uh, Michael. You can take it."

I go down to the bottom of the stairs, past my father, to take the phone.

"Hey, Chris. Yo. Hey," says Jerk.

"Hi, Jerk. How can I help you?"

"Man, how are you? I mean, what happened? I was really worried about you."

I ask sharply, "Why, Jerk? Why were you worried?"

"We were all worried. Rebecca was really worried about you."

I'm jumpy now. "Why? What did she say?"

"She said you, like, freaked out. She thought there was really something wrong with you."

"Oh god, no. She didn't."

"I mean, not like wrong with you wacko funny farm, but wrong with you, like something bad had happened. She said you were hiding your mouth and talking really weird."

"Oh, man. Oh. Damn!"

"What's the problem? Are you okay?"

"Did she say anything else?"

"I mean, she talked about it with Tom. He kind of explained that he'd been worried about you for the last couple of months, concerned 'cause he said you've been acting kind of, you know. Like he always says, that you've been acting like you have some problem."

"He said that to her? What did she say?"

"Then we heard that that girl you knew, you know, Lolli, the one from out of town, was a vampire. Did you hear? She, like, tried to kill Pete Gallagher. She was completely crazy. Man, it was horrible. He's in the hospital. They say he'll probably never play lacrosse again."

"What about Rebecca?"

"I don't know. She was really worried about you and stuff, especially after we heard about Lolli. And then Kristen started crying and Chuck put his arm around her, so Tom put his arm around Rebecca. They talked about how everything was so frightening, and how they were all really worried about you, and, you know, I left but I guess they all stayed out really late, sitting down by the reservoir, talking together about you and stuff. So I guess Tom and Rebecca are sort of, you know, like, going out now."

"*What*?" I scream. "He's doing this just to spite me! Isn't he? He's doing this just to spite me!"

"No," stutters Jerk nervously. "No, no he's not."

"That's why he's going out with her! Just to goddamn show me I can't! That bastard! Isn't that the reason?" I am in a fury. I pound my fist against the wall. My mother opens the door to the living room.

"Why are you out of your room?" she jabbers

anxiously, hanging back, as if ready to bolt. "Why are you out of your room? Get back to your room until I tell you to come out. Go on!" She gestures once, agitated, then ducks back into the living room.

Jerk waits for things to quiet down.

"Isn't that the reason?" I hiss. "For Tom."

He says, bewildered, "No. He's doing it because she's really nice. I talked to her for a while. She is. I mean, really nice. He's going out with her because she's really nice and interesting and stuff. She knows all this stuff about ancient spells and—"

"Thank you, Jerk," I say. "I really value your opinion."

"Look, Christopher—," he whines.

"What, Jerk. What else do you have to tell me?"

"I, I just called because I was worried about you, man."

"Worried? I'm really touched, Jerk. Your concern means so much to me. Like you understand what's going on. Like you understand any goddamn thing in the world."

"Hey!" he says. "I'm your friend. What are you—"

"Jerk, your only friend is your stupid dog. Your dog is so stupid. Why don't you go talk to your dog? It'll be sort of like your having a girlfriend, but the dog will have less chest hair."

"You," says Jerk. "You think I'm shit, don't you? Don't you? You just think I'm shit."

I sneer, "You are what you eat—" And instantly, I realize what I've done. And I can't believe it. "No, Jerk, I'm sorry. Please, Jerk, I'm sorry," I plead to the dial tone. "Jerk, I'm so sorry."

And now I am all alone.

I am up in my room.

I am grounded.

I am going to die soon.

The night has fallen, and the stars are out over the town. This is the town where I grew up. I grew up near the reservoir and used to play in the hills here. I don't want the life of that person who played in the hills and walked by the reservoir dragging a Tinkertoy ray gun to end. I want that person to be alive.

I someday want to go to exhibitions of spattered modern art with women with strict hairdos, and I want to murmur in their ears. I want to look out across the lake where I've bought my summer cottage and have arranged the playing cards in the phone desk drawer. I want to have memories of people laughing and driving in cars. I want to be alive in ten years to have a college pennant on the wall, and in twenty years to have a wife whose family I know well, and to have a microwave with a built-in convection oven with a two-year limited warranty. This is what is due to me, because I am an American; and I can't believe the thing I can feel squirming in my chest, that it is eating its way outward, and that I am going to be a killer.

I know that it is there, my vampiric heart, squelching in the cavern of my ribs, spitting and sucking blood. It will destroy me. It will.

As darkness grows thick around me and wraps itself on the furniture like black sheets hung in a house that will not be lived in again, I know that there is no hope and that there is nothing for me to do. My rage is wild and I am pacing around the room; I am pacing around it quickly because it is very small, and every moment it seems smaller.

Just tell my mother? Yes, yes, I think, because she will protect me in spite of everything. Mothers love their children, and she will protect me. It is only natural for mothers to love their children, it is the natural thing that always happens in the wild. Even with animals. Tonight on *Wild Kingdom*, "Mothers and Their Children." Natural. But—

Except that birds—and I remember—if a baby bird is touched by an alien hand—a human, a dog—and put back in its nest, the mother will peck it apart. She'll peck it to death because it's been touched.—I remember—when I was younger, a baby bird fell out of the nest, fell onto the ground; the other boys started throwing stones at it. I ran crying "Stop!" and took it in my hand (it was cheeping), but—

"You can't save it now," said one of my friends. "Its mother will kill it. She'll just kill it." He slapped my hand and made the chick fall out. Taking a rock, aiming at the sprawled chick, he said, "This is mercy."

He threw his rock. Its sharp edge hit the bird's eye, which popped like a blueberry. "This is mercy," he repeated, throwing another.

And the others picked up stones and hurled them. And even the little kids who were too little to understand the words repeated, again and again, as they flung their stones, "This is mercy!" "This is mercy!" (shrieking with laughter) "No, *this* is mercy!"

*Its mother will kill it. She'll just kill it.* I remember the changeling we heard about on TV, yowling in the fire. *It wasn't even human,* my mother said. *It wasn't even human.* And I'm coiled on my floor. Saliva drooping out of my lips. Teeth huge. Swollen. Hurting.

I'm hiding behind my door. It's near eleven. Television downstairs. Out in the night people are moving on the streets. Kids still playing kickball on the road by the streetlight. Footsteps shuffling along the hall.

I don't want anyone to knock. I don't want them to knock. When they do, I'll be tracing their blue veins in my mind from their fist up their arms, up to their necks, their soft, pulpy necks.

And suddenly, I love them because they are so fragile, because I am no longer one of them. And because I love them, I should run from them; run into the night and do the savage things I need to do.

No, I cannot do those things.

But I have to.

I don't know—no, I do know. I can't do those things. And I realize that the decision to be human is not one single instant, but is a thousand choices made every day. It is choices we make every second and requires constant vigilance. We have to fight to remain human.

And now I can't, now. (I'm huddled on my bed, rocking back and forth, my teeth gaping from my mouth. I moan while I rock.)

Shudders go through my body. My fingers grasp unseen objects and pull at them.

I'm hiding behind my stereo now. Don't want to see the light under the door.

Night is growing thick. House is dark. Sighing breaths rising and falling in soft white throats.

Three right here, right in this house.

And I'm hiding behind the doorway. There is no hope for me. That is all I know.

Hiding behind the doorway. Not that I would jump at someone who came in.

Not that I would jump.

I would never jump on a member of my family and drink their sweet, tart blood.

I would never.

Soon it will be the loneliest part of night.

Soon it will be the quiet hour.

My chin is wet.

Muscles twitch.

No, I think.

Don't do what you're.
Don't do.
No, please.
Behind the door.
I am thirsty.
I am thirsty.
Oh, god.
I am
so
thirsty